FESTIVAL FIASCO

A MAGICAL MANE MYSTERY

STELLA BIXBY

FERRY TAIL PUBLISHING LLC

This novel is a work of fiction. Names, characters, places, and incidents are either a product of the author's imagination or are used fictitiously. Any resemblance to actual persons, living or dead, businesses, events, or locales is entirely coincidental.

Copyright © 2022 by Crystal S. Ferry

All rights reserved.

No part of this book may be reproduced or transmitted in any form or by any means, electronic or mechanical, including photocopying, recording, or by any information storage and retrieval system presently available or yet to be invented without permission in writing from the publisher, except for the use of brief quotations in a book review.

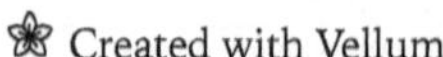 Created with Vellum

For My Readers

CAST OF CHARACTERS

Ellie - Main Character
Penelope - Ellie's Pet Pig
Mona - Ellie's VW Microbus
Esme - Ellie's Grandmother
Emily - Ellie's Mother
Harriet - Ellie's Cousin
Xander - Warlock/Laura's Boyfriend
Bernardo - Xander's Cousin/Ellie's Long-Distance Boyfriend
Jake - Police Chief/Emily's High School Sweetheart
Bex - Ellie's Best Friend/Works at Katie's Café
Katie - Married to Earl/Own's Katie's Café & Theater
Fran - Coupled with Amy/Own's Fran's Fabric & Feed
Amy - Coupled with Fran/Own's Amy's Antiques
Nancy - Married to Hank/Own's Nancy's Nails
Bonnie - Own's Helen's Hardware & Development Company
Renée - Widowed/Grand Witch of the States
Lucy - Ellie's Friend

Laura - Bex's Friend/Mayor for a Day Candidate
Georgia - Jake's Fiancée
Nick - Cliff Haven Mayor
Coral - Festival Planner
Deacon - Mayor for a Day Candidate
Andrea - Mayor for a Day Candidate
Susan - Mayor for a Day Candidate

1

The signs of spring were all around me—birds chirped, colorful flowers bloomed, all overlaid with the scents of dew-covered grass and—

Ugh. Dog poop.

"Wix," I grumbled my foster dog's name and pulled a poop bag out of my pocket to clean up the mess.

Wix always waited until we were in the town square to do his business. Maybe it was because of the nice grass. Or maybe it was just his natural pooping point.

Either way, every day I ended up carting a bag of dog doo all the way back to the house because the town refused to put out garbage cans.

I sighed.

Wix wasn't even my dog. I was his foster mom until they released his real mom from jail. I'd learned rather quickly, though, if I didn't take him on our morning run, he'd destroy everything in my house.

And I wasn't the kind of witch who knew how to use magic to clean up messes. Not yet, anyway.

"It's okay, buddy." I scratched Wix behind the ear as he looked up at me with his sweet brown eyes. "I just wish you could do your business at the house instead of in town."

Wix's gaze flashed away from me toward a squirrel darting up a tree.

Before I could command him not to chase it, he was yanking me along behind him, a full poop bag swinging from my hand.

"Wix, stop," I finally managed, and he did. Right in front of me.

I toppled over him, landing on my shoulder.

The smell hit me before I registered the warm squishiness on my arm.

I hadn't tied the bag before Wix had taken off after the squirrel.

Without having to look, I knew the poop was now smashed between my arm, hand, and the ground.

My gag reflex took over. Thankfully, I hadn't eaten, and nothing made its way from my stomach to the ground.

Wix sniffed me once, then backed away. Whether he could smell his own poop or the frustration rising in my chest, I wasn't sure.

If the town just had trash cans, I might have been able to throw it away before it ended up all over me.

"Are you all right?" A deep voice I was all too familiar with came from behind me, making me want to sink into the ground for eternity.

I turned to see Xander and Laura walking hand in hand toward me.

I gagged for a second time, though I wasn't certain it

was because of the poop that was now melding with my skin.

"Ellie?" Xander asked again as Wix began sniffing him all over.

"I'm fine," I said. "Nothing to see here. Go on and enjoy your morning walk."

Laura wrinkled her nose. "What's that awful smell?"

"Can I help you up?" Xander asked, releasing Laura's hand and reaching for mine.

Wix growled low. He'd never liked Xander.

I stayed plastered to the ground. "No, that's okay. I'm —um—doing some yoga."

"Yoga?" Xander asked. "But your hair is bright red. Isn't yoga supposed to make you feel calm? Shouldn't your hair be blue or even just white?"

Why did he have to notice my hair? I knew I should have pulled it into a bun and tucked it under a cap today.

"Did you fart?" Laura asked with a giggle. "I hear yoga makes you fart."

"No," I said. "I did not fart. I don't know what the smell is. But please, just keep going on your walk."

"Seriously, El, let me help you up." Xander shoved his hand closer to me.

"I'm fine," I said through gritted teeth. "Keep walking. There's nothing to see here."

"Are you hurt and don't want to tell us?" Xander asked.

"Maybe she pooped her pants," Laura said, pinching her nose. "That smell is definitely more than just a fart."

"I did not poop my pants." I must have turned over just enough for them to see what was going on because they both gasped in horror at what I assumed looked like I'd rolled in dog poop. Which was basically the truth.

"What kind of weird yoga requires you to roll around in dog poop?" Laura asked, narrowing her eyes at me. "It's a magical cult, isn't it?"

Xander turned to look at her. "It's not a magical cult."

She glanced at him. "Sorry."

Laura and her entire family hated magic. That is until Xander appeared on the scene. Apparently, good looks trumped the fact that he was a warlock.

"I tripped over Wix when he went after a squirrel and ended up in this . . . predicament."

Xander no longer had a hand outstretched for me. But I didn't need his help to get on my feet.

I did my best not to look down at the mess covering my arm. "I think we'll head home so I can shower. Then I'm coming back to town to talk to the mayor about getting some garbage cans in the square."

"Why don't you come to the town meeting tonight?" Xander asked.

Laura elbowed him in the ribs.

"What?" he asked.

"I'm sure Ellie has more important things to do than to come to a silly town meeting." Laura sneered at me.

"They're actually kind of fun," Xander said. "Lots of drama."

"I can bring up trash cans at the town meeting?" I asked.

"Sure," Xander said. "Then everyone can vote on it, and they can be approved right away."

"There are more steps than that," Laura said.

"It's better than storming the mayor's office covered in poop," Xander said.

"I was going to shower first," I said. "But maybe if I did go covered in poop, the mayor would get the hint more quickly."

Xander laughed.

"The mayor isn't someone you want to mess with," Laura said. "He got elected on his good looks and charm, but underneath all that, he's a snake in the grass. We went to high school together. Let's just say he wasn't very nice."

"I think I can handle him," I said. "But maybe I'll do it the proper way and come to the meeting."

Laura scowled as if she knew she'd just practically talked me into coming. Why she didn't want me there was beyond me. Probably because she didn't want me any more ingrained in the town than I already was.

"We can give you a ride home," Xander said.

"Uh, no we can't." Laura looked at him as if he'd grown another head. "She's not getting in my brand new car smelling like that."

"It's okay," I said. "I can run home. Wix needs the exercise, or he'll destroy all of my pillows."

"You're going to run home covered in dog poop?" Xander looked me up and down. "At least let me use my magic to clean it up."

Laura glared at him.

"But," he said as if asking for her permission.

She shook her head.

A torn expression came over his face as he looked from her to me and back again.

"I'll be okay," I said. "The wind will take away the smell. I'll just pretend it's mud or something."

Xander looked at Laura again with a pleading expression, but she just stood there with her arms across her chest.

"It's really okay," I said.

Xander's loyalty had to be with his girlfriend. He had chosen her, after all. Not that I hadn't been forming some sort of relationship with his cousin. But long-distance wasn't really my thing.

"Come on, Wix. Let's head home." I tugged on his lead, and he trotted after me. "See you guys at the town meeting."

I could feel Xander's eyes on me as I did my best to hold my head high, knowing I looked as bad as I smelled.

I would get those garbage cans in the square, even if I had to pay for them myself.

I scrubbed for nearly an hour, but the smell of poop lingered in my nostrils long after the shower. It had been so caked into my clothes I'd simply tossed them in the garbage. The sweatpants had holes in them, anyway.

Wix was passed out on the couch when I returned downstairs.

Penelope—my pet pig and best friend in the entire world—trotted behind me to the kitchen. I pushed the bottom of the island, where a magical sparkle waited for me to reveal the hidden staircase beneath.

I'd never heard of town meetings before, but I suspected my grandmother—Esme—likely had and possibly kept notes about them in her study.

When I'd inherited the farm, barn, and farmhouse, I had no idea how magical it was. Eventually, I realized it was more magical than I could have imagined. The pond out back was only visible to a magical eye, the mural in the barn—now my therapeutic recreation studio—changed of its own accord, the wreath of lilacs on my bedroom door never died, and the rooms chose who they allowed to sleep in them.

And then there were the secret spaces—the attic and the basement—both with their own energies and purposes.

The attic was a place of warmth and reflection. Esme left her personal journal for me alongside a cozy chair. Penelope and I spent a great deal of time up there reading through the parts of the journal that revealed themselves to me. I'd also recently begun writing my own entries in the back.

The basement was Esme's study—the place she kept her books and notes about cases she worked on. It was dark but not damp, like most basements. The plaster walls glowed with warm light, illuminating heavy beams that extended across the ceiling.

As an orphan hopping in and out of foster homes, I never would have imagined the life I had now.

Once deep within the basement, I slid into a chair behind one of the polished wooden desks and pulled out a notebook I'd only peeked inside once before. Esme had taken extensive notes about all the criminal cases with which she helped the police. I'd gone through and filed most of them along one of the bookshelves lining the wall.

But this notebook had details about the town. The first page listed all the town shops—Katie's Café, Nancy's Nails, Helen's Hardware, and a bunch more. Helen's Hardware was still called Helen's Hardware, but Helen had since died, and Bonnie had taken over the business in her place.

As I flipped through the pages, I finally came to some dated entries.

The first was definitely from a town meeting.

Nancy wanted to put a new sign outside her building—something more eye-catching. Belinda made a huge fuss about how everyone would have to update their signs if one person did and how it would make the town look less authentic. The mayor agreed to let Nancy paint her sign with the same colors to make it fresher. Then told everyone else they were free to do the same thing with their signs. Belinda threw a fit claiming Nancy needed to pay for the paint. When the mayor disagreed, Belinda stood up and walked out in record time. Usually she at least lasted through the voting.

I giggled, thinking about the women I'd grown to love like my own family arguing over their signs. Then realized they'd probably still argue about the same thing to this day. I flipped a few more pages until I came to one with an all-caps heading.

INTRUDER SPY

Someone from Poppy Hills came to the town meeting tonight to declare war on Cliff Haven.

War? My heart rate raced as I continued to read.

The strawberry field on the edge of town has always been in Cliff Haven. The town line says so. At least the majority of it has. For crying in the mud, we host the Cliff Haven Strawberry Festival every year. But this INTRUDER SPY came into our town meeting today to announce that they wouldn't be allowing the strawberries grown within their town limits to be used in our Strawberry Festival. Which means we'd have to find strawberries from another town because all of the strawberries are within their town limits. In fact, they're planning on hosting their own Strawberry Festival this year. With our strawberries. Of course, the farm owner won't stand up to them. Probably because they're holding some permitting stuff over her head. The Strawberry Festival is ruined.

Strawberry festival? This was the first I'd heard about a Strawberry Festival. Which probably meant it was no longer a Cliff Haven event.

I closed the journal and sat back in the chair. Asking for trash cans in the square shouldn't be an issue. Who wouldn't want trash cans? It wasn't like I was coming from another town trying to take a beloved event away.

3

"That's a no on the trash cans. Onto the next complaint?" Nick—the Cliff Haven mayor and a man in his thirties who I'd never met—stood at a podium at the front of the large, but crowded, room. It seemed everyone came to town meetings—everyone but me.

"Wait," I said, standing. "That's it?"

The people surrounding me gaped as if Nick's word was gospel.

Nick sighed, his chiseled chest muscles visible through his thin t-shirt. You'd think a mayor would dress more appropriately for a town meeting. The group of women wearing low-cut blouses in the front row hinted that the good turnout might have been more about Nick's looks than official town matters.

"We don't have the budget for trash cans in the square. Now, let's move on to—"

"I'll buy them," I said.

Katie smiled up at me.

"Will you take them out every day too?" Nick asked, his tone condescending. "And keep the town stocked with trash bags? And what about if they get vandalized? Will you be the one to repaint them or buy new ones? There's far more to consider than the simple purchase of the cans."

I guess I hadn't completely thought it through. "I think it would help our town stay cleaner."

"Are you saying the town is dirty?" he asked.

"No, but—"

"Because if you think the town is dirty, you need to take that up with the Chief of Police."

Jake—the Chief of Police—was my unofficial father-type figure, or "faux-father," as we called it. He'd dated my mother in high school. That was before she'd run away to have me, left me at a fire station, and then disappeared.

"I don't think the town is dirty," I said, glancing at Jake, who sat next to his fiancée, Georgia. "I'd just like a place to throw out my foster dog's poop after I pick it up."

"I assumed you could wave your magic wand and poof it away." Nick's tone was mean in the way Laura's was when she spoke about my magic. "Do you not have a trash can at your house?"

I could feel my blood pressure rising and the tingling in my scalp changing my hair color. "Of course, I have a trash can at my house," I said as calmly as I could. "But my house is miles from the town square."

"That is not the town's issue," Nick said. "It is your choice to bring your dog miles from your home to defecate in the town square. Now, if you would kindly sit down so we can continue with our business."

The women in the front row all nodded up at Nick in agreement.

Xander glanced back at me and mouthed an apology as Laura's shoulders jolted with laughter.

Everything in me wanted to storm out of the room, but Katie gently grabbed my hand and pulled me back into my seat.

Laura turned and whispered, "He probably just doesn't like the way you smell. Did you even take a shower?"

Tears flooded my eyes. I thought I was the only one who could still smell the poop on me. I'd even used perfume—something I rarely did.

"You turn around and mind your own business," Katie hissed, her mama bear tendencies coming out. "There's no need to be nasty."

I wiped the tears from my eyes, determined not to let them fall down my cheeks.

"Don't mind her," Katie whispered in my ear. "You don't smell *that* bad."

Her words didn't make me feel any better. Instead, they confirmed what I already feared—I still reeked of dog poop.

"Let's move onto the Strawberry Festival," the mayor said.

My head whipped up so fast I nearly gave myself whiplash.

"Since long-time Cliff Haven residents have graciously purchased the strawberry farm, we will finally get the festival back from Poppy Hills."

Cheers erupted, the loudest coming from the front row groupies.

"This means we'll be taking nominations for Mayor for a Day candidates." He looked around the room. "Would anyone like to begin?"

From directly in front of me, Xander stood. "I'd like to nominate Laura."

My heart twisted in my chest. I hated that I still had feelings for him.

Laura stood and smiled sweetly at everyone, then leaned over and kissed Xander on his cheek. "Thanks, babe."

"Can I nominate myself?" Someone asked near the front.

"I don't believe you can," Nick said. "Let me just check."

While he checked the official rule book, I leaned over to Katie and whispered, "Nominate me."

"Why?"

"I need those trash cans," I said. "If I become Mayor for a Day, I'll make my order of business to change the budget to include trash cans and everything they require."

"Is that the only reason?" She glanced at Laura and Xander. He had his arm around her shoulder.

"It's the only reason," I hissed.

She shrugged. "All right."

"The rules state you cannot nominate yourself," Nick finally said. "I'm sorry."

"I'd like to nominate Susan." A man stood and smiled at who I suspected was Susan.

Susan stood, her face bright red. "Thank you, Deacon."

Nick's face turned sour. "Anyone else?"

Katie stood. "I'd like to nominate someone to whom I will personally give my vote—Ellie Vanderwick."

Several people gasped.

I rose from my seat. "I accept your nomination, Katie. I only hope everyone else can see the value in trash cans like I can."

"We aren't here to campaign," Nick growled.

"I'm not campaigning," I said. "I'm simply acknowledging there's a problem that I intend to solve."

"We'll see about that," he said. "Are there any other nominations?"

"I'd like to nominate my best friend Andrea," Susan said.

A woman with long brown hair and a serious face stood. "I accept the nomination."

"Fantastic," Nick said between gritted teeth. He didn't seem thrilled with any of the candidates. Well, other than Laura. He didn't seem too perturbed that she'd been nominated.

A gray-haired woman in the front row stood. "My name is Darla, and I'd like to nominate my son, Deacon."

The man who had nominated Susan stood with a smug look on his clean-shaven face. "I accept the nomination." He turned and looked directly at me, sending a shiver down my spine.

Deacon held my gaze as he lowered himself back into his seat, then slowly turned back around to face the front of the room.

"Do you know him?" Katie asked.

I shook my head. "I don't think so."

"Because he was staring straight at you."

"Do you?"

She squinted. "I can't say I do."

This surprised me. Katie knew practically everyone. She made it her business to.

"Maybe he's new in town," she said.

"And already wants to be Mayor for a Day?" I asked.

"Any more nominations?" Nick asked.

No one stood.

"If that's it, we have Deacon, Andrea, Laura, Susan, and Ellie," the mayor said, practically choking on the last two names. "The five of you will be required to attend every mayoral preparation meeting in the coming days. If you miss even one, you will be removed from candidacy."

Maybe I was being paranoid, but I could have sworn he directed his comment at me.

4

After the meeting concluded, I found myself in front of a potluck spread worthy of a holiday gathering.

"Are all the meetings like this?" I asked Katie, who was filling a plate next to me.

"Since Nick was elected mayor, they have been," she said.

"When was he elected?" I asked. Usually, I knew about these types of things.

"Not long before you came to town."

"Then why haven't I heard about him? Or these meetings?" I added a heaping pile of mashed potatoes to my plate next to the turkey and corn casserole.

"I believe that's because I didn't want you here," Nick's voice came from behind me.

I turned and gaped at him. "What do you mean, you didn't want me here?" I glanced at Katie, who wouldn't meet my eye.

"It's nothing personal," Nick said. He was handsome

in an over-the-top sort of way. "I just think town meetings should be reserved for people who truly exude town pride."

"And you don't think I exude town pride?"

"How could you?" His tone was light, but there was a hint of animosity there. "You just moved here."

"So you didn't want me to come to the meetings because I just moved here? Or is it because I'm a witch?"

He narrowed his eyes at me. "That certainly doesn't help the matter."

Katie stepped between the two of us. "Nick, do I need to speak to your mother about your behavior?"

"Oh, please do, Miss Katie," he said. "I'm sure she'll be on my side. Especially when it comes to the Vanderwicks."

I couldn't believe what I was hearing. Did I not pay taxes just like everyone else?

"Perhaps if she'd walked in here intending to help at her first meeting, rather than asking for something straight away, I'd have been more inclined to proper manners."

"If I'd have known there were town meetings, I'd have come sooner and wouldn't have had to find out about them because I—the town—had a need." I held my ground. This man seemed to get what he wanted—*whatever* he wanted. Men like that frustrated me. Set me on edge.

"I hope you know what you're getting into with the Mayor for a Day candidacy. It's a stringent process. Perhaps more stringent than trash cans warrant?" He started to walk away but then turned back and said, "Do save some mashed potatoes for the rest of the townspeople."

He was gone before I could come up with a reply. When I glanced down at my plate, it was piled high with the potatoes I'd apparently been scooping spoonful after spoonful upon as he spoke.

Katie giggled beside me.

"It's not funny," I said, unable to stop the laughter bubbling in my throat. It was kind of funny. At least the potatoes were. And how seriously he was taking this Mayor for a Day thing.

"What do you know about the Mayor for a Day candidacy?" I asked.

We took our plates—mine weighing a verifiable ton—to one of the circular tables behind the rows of folding chairs we'd been sitting in for the meeting.

"Maybe you should have looked into it before you forced me to nominate you," Katie said with a quirked eyebrow.

"I didn't force you," I said. "Plus, you said I have your vote."

"You'd have my vote for anything. You know that. But this is going to be a challenge. Many people won't see trash cans as a necessity."

"Does no one else walk their dogs in the square?" I asked. "Has no one else had to deal with cleaning up their pooch's excrement?"

She shrugged. "The only people I know who have dogs live on farms or have yards."

"But you know everyone," I said, then placed my fork

alongside my plate. "Maybe trash cans aren't that important."

"If they're important to you, they're important," Katie said. "We'll just have to figure out how to convince the rest of the town."

"We?"

"You didn't think I'd leave you to do this yourself, did you?"

"I don't—"

"I'd never do that." Katie placed a hand over mine. "We're going to win this race. Just like you won the Trot 'n Tater. Now get to those potatoes. You and I both know you have the stomach to finish them."

I laughed more for her sake than my own. With Katie invested, I couldn't go running away with my tail between my legs. Not that I had it in me to do that, anyway. Competition ran through my blood even when I wished it didn't.

"That's a lot of taters," Laura said, sitting in the chair next to me. Xander sat on the other side of her. "You training for a marathon or something?"

"Laura," Katie warned.

"I'm just stating the obvious," she said. "It's not every day someone eats an entire field-full of potatoes in one sitting."

"I'm heading home," I said to Katie before standing. "We can chat tomorrow."

I took my full plate with me to Mona—my Volkswagen Microbus—ignoring the giggles coming from behind me. I wasn't hungry anymore, but I was confident between Penelope and Wix, the food wouldn't go to waste.

"Looking for a garbage can to dispose of your wasted food?"

I whipped around to see Nick standing in the middle of a group of women—the ones from the front row.

"I'm taking it home with me," I said.

Andrea stepped forward from the group and said, "I'm looking forward to going against you in the Mayor for a Day race."

Magic edged her features, though I wasn't sure whether anyone else knew she was a witch. However, that might explain why Nick didn't seem thrilled that she'd been nominated for Mayor for a Day.

"I am, too," I said. "Thanks."

She went back to the group, standing between Nick and Susan.

Deacon stood off in the shadows, his gaze focused on me.

I shook off the anxious feeling I got from him and locked myself inside Mona. If it wasn't for the faint smell of dog poop wafting around me, I might have simply thrown in the towel on the whole Mayor for a Day thing.

5

Katie and several other women from the community met me in the barn the next morning. We'd been doing yoga every other morning for the past month. Though they grumbled, they'd all gotten stronger and more agile—the overall goal of the yoga classes.

Growing up, I'd always known I wanted to help people, but it wasn't until I was in college I realized I could combine my love of fitness and recreation with therapy to help increase others' quality of life. No one would have thought the poor little orphan girl with terrifying color-changing hair would make anything of herself, but here I was.

It didn't hurt that I'd been gifted a place to live and enough money to sustain me for the rest of my life, but still. I liked to think I would have grown my business without the inheritance.

"Trash cans, huh?" Fran—the owner of Fran's Feed,

Fabric, and Flowers—asked as she and her partner, Amy, walked in. "That's the hill you want to die on?"

"If you'd have seen what happened, you'd want trash cans too," I said.

"I didn't have to see it," Fran said. "Laura gave practically everyone in town a vivid account."

"I'm sure she did," I said.

"Is she still worried you'll take Xander from her?" Bonnie—the new owner of Helen's Hardware—asked.

I scoffed at the notion. "Xander's smitten with her. He chose her."

"That's one way to look at it," Katie said. "The other is that you chose his scruffy foreign cousin over him."

We'd had this disagreement so many times it was becoming almost a morning tradition.

"Either way," I said. "I won't try to take Xander from Laura. I don't need to take a man. If a man wants to be with me, he should choose to be with me without coercion."

"Magical or otherwise." Fran winked.

"For the last time, I can't control other people's emotions with my magic," I said.

They all laughed.

"Let's finish our coffee and get our mats out," I said. "I have somewhere to be this morning."

"Oh, did you get the schedule, too?" Katie asked. "I practically had to rip it from Nick's hands last night as I was leaving. I didn't think he'd be so quick to give it to you."

"Nick didn't give me any schedule," I said. "I have a meeting with Lucy."

"You'll have to reschedule," Katie said. "Nick has Mayor for a Day training all day today."

"Already?" I asked.

"The festival is in less than a week," Katie said.

"How is the town supposed to plan an entire festival in less than a week?" I asked.

"It's not like they just started planning," Fran said. "I hear they hired some big wig from the city to plan it."

"Not a Cliffer?" I asked. Cliffers were what we called Cliff Haven residents.

Fran shrugged.

"Did Nick grow up here?" I asked as I started leading the stretches.

"His family has lived here longer than most," Fran said.

"Are they like Laura's family, where they all hate magical people?" I asked.

"Laura doesn't seem to hate magical people," Fran said with a laugh. "At least not the male variety."

"No," Katie said, ignoring Fran's comment. "They're not like Laura's family. There's just always been a rift there."

"What happened?" I asked, lifting my arms over my head, then bending toward the floor.

"I've no idea," Katie said.

The others shrugged, too.

"But I do know, you have to go to that training today. I'm sure Lucy will understand," Katie said.

Lucy had been teaching me more about my magical abilities. She and Renée—the temporary Grand Witch of the States—were trying to convince me I'd needed to take my place as the next Grand Witch. My grandmother had been the last Grand Witch until she'd passed. With my mother missing, I was next in line. Sort of like royalty only without the crown.

Maybe if there had been a crown, I'd have been more inclined—

"Ellie?" Katie asked. "Are we going to stay like this for much longer?"

We were in a downward dog position. "Sorry," I said. "Let's move into upward dog."

The women let out exhales, their faces red from the slight inversion.

"I'll have to get showered after this," I said. "Then I can pick you up for the training."

"Oh no," Katie said. "I must not have been clear. I can't go to the training. Only Mayor for a Day candidates can."

Perfect, so I'd be stuck with Nasty Nick and Lousy Laura all day. "How many of these trainings do I have to do?"

"Only a few," Katie said. "And then there are the interviews, the debates, headshots, and the final speeches at the actual festival."

"Sounds like an awful lot for some measly trash cans," Fran said. "If you need to throw your poo bags away, you can put them in the dumpster behind Amy's."

Amy's was actually Amy's Antiques—one of the businesses on the square. Amy and Fran's apartment was on the second floor, above the antique shop.

"What about everyone else?" I asked. "You don't want a bunch of poo bags in your dumpster."

"Everyone else who?" Fran asked. "I sell dog food to every dog owner in town. Do you know what I don't sell? Poo bags. Except to you. And thank goodness for that. I bought a bunch years ago and thought I'd have to toss them."

"So what do people do with their dogs' poop?"

"We already discussed this," Katie said. "No one takes their dogs to the square but you. No one."

"Well, towns need trash cans," I said. "In Colorado, there were trash cans on every street corner."

"Sweetie," Katie said. "You're not in Colorado anymore. Things are different here in Iowa. Plus, if everyone picked up their own trash, what would Jake's guys do?"

"Who exactly are these guys I keep hearing about?" I asked.

"Jake's guys are the local inmates. You know, the ones who aren't going to prison but still have to be in jail. It's part of their community service."

"Couldn't their community service be to empty the trash cans and then do something else?" I asked. "I mean, if they're already paying for the bags and there are workers, we'd just need to buy the cans. Why is that such a stretch?"

Katie smiled. "You don't have to convince us. You need to convince the rest of the town."

"Yeah," Fran said. "You already have our votes."

I smiled. I'd go to that Mayor for a Day training and be the best possible student. Then I'd get the rest of the town's votes.

As I was straightening the yoga mats and making sure everything was ready for the next session, something moved from the corner of my eye. I pushed the last rolled-up mat into its cubby and made my way to the back of the barn, where I thought I'd seen something.

The mural was as it had been for nearly a week straight and on and off for the past couple of months—the diner. When I'd first found the magical mural in the back of my barn, it had been of the farm—the barn and the house—and people.

They started out being simply three women with white hair and their backs toward me, which I took to be my mother, grandmother, and me. But as time went on, the people changed to include the rest of the town, Jake, and my cousin—Harriet.

It wasn't until recently that the background changed to this diner that I'd never seen in real life.

Regardless of what the mural showed, my mother's name—Emily Vanderwick—was always scrawled at the bottom. This was her mural—her magical mural—and it gave me hope that somewhere she was still alive.

I took another step toward the back wall, searching for additional movement. The painting had never moved before as I watched, though there had been a time when a speck of magic had been on the surface.

The diner seemed much like it usually did with unrecognizable figures inside enjoying their meals and a waitress or two serving coffee and food—their features hidden by their turned heads.

But something was different. Usually, the diner appeared with a light sky behind the trees that formed a line in the background. Not tonight. Tonight, the sky was a dark blue—almost black. Tiny stars seemed to glisten in the sky, but the moon was nowhere to be seen.

I reached up to touch the stars. Maybe they were little magical stars. But when my finger came in contact, they were just as smooth as the rest of the painted wood.

I slid my finger down the board. Just as I was about to lift it, it stopped on a window I'd never seen before. A basement window.

The familiar sensation of magic twisting up my arm made me tense up in expectation of being thrown into a vision of sorts. The last time I'd touched a magical speck on the mural, my mind had gone to an underground tunnel with a train coming straight at me.

This time, though, I stayed fully conscious as I watched the mural move before my very eyes. The customers moved as if they were taking bites of their food, chatting with each other, and drinking their coffee. A light in the window—the basement window—flickered on and off, on and off.

I waited for it to turn back on, but it didn't.

My finger was stuck to that window as if the magic was holding it there. Was this some sort of magical plea for help?

Maybe this was a real diner, and someone was trapped in the basement.

My gaze darted all around, searching for another clue.

The waitresses moved around delivering plates as a couple walked out of the diner and got into their car.

When my gaze returned to the diner windows, a waitress had her hands cupped around her eyes, looking out.

My breath caught in my chest.

It was like looking in a mirror.

Other than the eyes and a few extra wrinkles, the woman in the window looked just like me.

6

My finger stayed on the mural as the woman I assumed to be my mother peered outside the diner. Could she see me? Was this something like a two-way magic mirror? Or magical spyglass or something?

Confusion spread over Emily's face as she pulled back and shook her head.

"Mom?" I called, the word unfamiliar in my mouth. "Er—Emily?"

The woman turned her back to me and continued pouring coffee as if she hadn't seen me at all.

Then a flash of something startled me. As I jolted backward and my finger lifted from the wall, the mural went blurry with the motion. The diner was still in focus, but the car that the couple had gotten into looked like a streak across the bottom as it had sped away.

I pushed my finger back to the paint, hoping to make it come back to life, but it stayed as it was. A mess. This wasn't the work of my brilliant painter mother. This was the work of newbie magic—my newbie magic.

I sighed. I'd seen her. And she might have seen me, too. All I knew was I needed to find this diner, and soon.

Nick stood with his hands on his hips, staring at a chalkboard. The school was small, but the rooms were jam-packed together. I had a hard time finding my way to the proper classroom until a teenage girl reluctantly pointed me in the right direction.

Why we had a Mayor for a Day training class at the actual school rather than the Town Hall was beyond me.

"Just in time," Nick said without turning around. "Has anyone taught you, Miss Vanderwick, that early is on time and on time is late?"

"I'm early," I said, glancing down at my phone screen to check. "I still have three minutes to spare."

He turned and focused his piercing blue gaze on me. "And that's why I'm not kicking you out of the class. Please, sit."

So much for being the best student. I pushed my shoulders back and took a seat in the front row. He probably expected me to cower and take a back-row seat, but he didn't know who he was dealing with.

Laura, Susan, Deacon, and Andrea sat at various places in the room, each with a notebook and pen to take notes. Thankfully, Katie had sent me prepared with my very own backpack full of goodies.

"We'll begin with the history of Cliff Haven," Nick said. "Take notes. This will be on the test."

"You have to be kidding, Nick," Susan said with a glare.

"I'm not kidding, *Susan*," he said her name with more animosity than he'd put into any word he'd spoken to me. "The town deserves a mayor who takes pride in Cliff Haven. Even if that mayor is only in the position for a day."

"Just because you take it so seriously doesn't mean that's what the town wants." Susan was not backing down.

"They elected me, didn't they?" Nick said.

"I believe the margin was rather narrow," Andrea said from behind me. "And you refused a recount."

I glanced over my shoulder. She wore a red pantsuit that looked like it belonged in Washington D.C. And I thought I was overdressed in my black slacks and pink button-down blouse.

"I voted for you," Susan said to Andrea.

Andrea barely glanced in Susan's direction when she said, "Forgive me if I'm not terribly flattered that you'd vote for me over your ex-husband."

I whipped around to see Nick rubbing his left temple with his fingertips. He and Susan had been married, and he'd run against Andrea for the mayoral position.

Neither Laura nor Deacon looked surprised by any of this.

"Perhaps if you take this class seriously, you'll win the next election," Nick said to Andrea.

She didn't look even slightly fazed by him.

"We'll start at the beginning—when Cliff Haven was founded," Glen said.

But he didn't get a chance to go on before a tiny woman with bright red hair, green eyes, and a magical glisten burst into the room. "You started without me?"

"You're late," Nick said, pointing at the clock.

"Looks like I'm right on time," the woman said with a smile, then turned to the class. "I'm Coral Bell, the event planner."

Nick looked furious that Coral had interrupted his history lesson, but he didn't interrupt her.

Coral turned to the door and waved a beckoning arm, "Come on in."

Three teenage boys walked in carrying large plastic totes.

"You can just leave them here," Cora said, batting her long black eyelashes. "Thank you for your help."

They blushed and left the room.

"What is all this?" Nick asked.

"These candidates don't need your silly history lesson," she said. "They need to make the festival look good. And to make the festival look good, they're going to need flashy signs, good speeches, and beautiful headshots."

She began removing the lids from the totes, revealing mounds and mounds of craft supplies.

"While I'm setting everything out," Coral said to Nick, "can you write everyone's campaign platforms on the whiteboard?"

Nick did not look thrilled to be reduced to Coral's assistant but did as she asked, anyway.

"We all know what Ellie's is," Nick said. He wrote one word—*trash*—under my name.

Laura snickered.

I ignored his childish jab.

"Who's next?" Nick asked. "Susan?"

I was surprised he picked his ex-wife as the next person.

"I want that ridiculous statue taken down."

Nick gaped at her. "What statue?"

"You know what statue," she said.

"My statue?" Nick asked. "You want my statue taken down? But you helped me choose it."

"Some good that did," Susan said.

"I did not cheat on you with that woman," Nick said. "She's from Poppy Hills. And I never cheated. I wouldn't stoop to your level."

"Okay, that's enough," Andrea said. "That's what she's campaigning for. Write it on the board."

Nick looked at Andrea, then at Susan, then back at Andrea.

"Just write it down," Coral said. "We don't have all day."

Nick's head looked like it might explode at any moment. But he did as Coral said.

"While you're writing, add mine," Andrea said. "If I win, I'm going to abolish the mayoral position in Cliff Haven."

Cue head explosion in three, two, one . . .

Nick turned around slowly.

My heart pounded in my chest.

Every part of me wanted to crack a joke. Or run out of the room. But I couldn't. I had to stay.

Why?

For trash cans?

That seemed absurd at the moment.

"You want to abolish my position?" Nick whispered.

"It makes sense for the town," Andrea said.

Susan looked concerned for her friend.

"You just ran for the mayoral office," Nick said.

"And I would have had the perfect position to get rid of it if I'd been elected," Andrea said. "But alas, I must do it this way instead."

"That's not within the realm of the Mayor for a Day's authority," Nick said.

"I guess we'll have to wait and see." Andrea shrugged. "That is if I'm elected."

Nick caught Coral giving him the side-eye, turned, and wrote Andrea's platform on the board. "Laura, what's yours?" he asked without turning around.

"I want to increase the budget for town decorations," she said.

"See?" Nick turned around and pointed at Susan, then Andrea. "Why can't you two pick something nice like that?"

"Nick," Coral said.

He grumbled something under his breath before turning back to the whiteboard and writing Laura's perfectly wholesome platform on the board under her name.

"Deacon, what's yours?" Nick asked.

"I'd like to lower taxes," Deacon said.

Nick let out a burst of laughter, then stopped himself when he realized Deacon wasn't joking. "In one day? You're going to lower taxes in one day? It's Mayor for a Day. The keyword being—*day*."

Deacon glared at Nick. "Just write it down."

"I'm not writing that down," Nick said. "It's absurd. You know you can't just lower taxes. What's your real motive? It's a bait and switch, isn't it? You're going to get everyone to vote for you, then do something outlandish on your day, right?"

Deacon said nothing.

"What's your real motive?" Nick asked. "Other than sleeping with my wife?"

"Ex-wife," Andrea said.

Nick didn't look at her.

If only I could hide under my desk, I would. I had no idea getting trash cans would be so difficult. Or so dramatic.

"I want to lower taxes," Deacon finally said. "That's my platform. Write it down."

"Just write it," Coral said. "We have things to do."

Nick did as instructed.

"Good," Coral said, a bubbly smile breaching her lips. "Now that we all know each other's platforms, we can make slander posters against one another."

A nervous laugh bubbled up my neck and escaped my lips.

"That seems unnecessary," Susan said. "Can't we just make posters about our own platforms instead?"

"That's no fun," Coral said. "This is more than just a Mayor for a Day race. It's a publicity generator. The harsher the posters, the more people will become invested in the race. The more they're invested in the race, the more money they'll spend at the festival. Isn't that the goal? For people to spend money at the festival?"

Nick nodded. "That and the tradition of it all."

"Right," Coral said. "Let's get to it."

She made us sit as far away from one another as possible as she handed out supplies.

"We will reveal these posters at the debates," she said. "No sharing until then. I'd encourage you to pick just one candidate that you think is your biggest opponent and focus on them."

The others seemed almost excited to create their slander posters. I was not. There was absolutely no way I could make a poster that focused negatively on someone else. Coral would probably get angry, but I had to stick to my guns on this one.

"Do you have any green slime?" Laura asked. "Like the color of trash?"

My head popped up, and our gazes met. She was making her slander poster about me.

"No slime," Coral said. "But I have green glitter."

"That'll work," Laura said with an evil smirk at me.

Anger tingled my scalp, but I couldn't let it get to me. I would not retaliate. They could all slander me and my trash can idea, but I wouldn't play into this stupid game. No matter how much publicity it might generate.

Then, I got an idea.

What if I slandered myself? Make a joke of it? I mean, asking for trash cans was kind of ridiculous.

I started on my poster, eager to get my ideas on paper.

Coral started around the room, oohing and ahhing over everyone's work. When she reached Susan's, she whispered something that made Deacon's head pop up. Whatever Coral had said to Susan seemed to upset Deacon as his face wrinkled into a frown.

When he caught me watching, he gave me one of his evil looks that sent sparks of warning to my scalp. What was it about him that made my hair send out red flags?

He seemed perfectly okay in his black slacks, matching jacket, and dark red tie with tiny white polka dots. His hair was neatly combed. His face was clean-shaven. There was nothing about him that screamed danger. Well, except the fact that every time he looked at me, I wanted to get as far as humanly possible away from him.

"That's an interesting choice, Ellie," Coral said, making me jump in my seat.

Deacon turned slowly back to his own poster.

"I just couldn't—"

"Hush," Coral said. "I understand."

I smiled down at my work. It might not get me elected, but it also didn't go against my values.

7

I took the lunch Katie packed me out on the front lawn of the school the second Coral dismissed us. I had no idea where everyone else went, but they hadn't followed me. I made sure to watch behind me. Especially for Deacon.

The students, however, were also out for lunch. Some of them loitered around on the grass eating and chatting, while others walked out to their cars and headed deeper into town, probably to stop at Katie's Café for a quick burger.

I was halfway into my sandwich when I saw Laura approaching.

"You won't get elected, you know." Laura sat on the grass in front of me.

I shrugged. "We'll see."

"He hates you," she said. "There's no way he'll let you and your garbage can campaign go through."

"I don't know that Nick is the one in charge at this

point." I took a bite of the heavenly pasta salad in front of me.

"I guess we'll see," she said, standing. "I'm going to eat my lunch inside."

I wanted to yell at her as she walked away—*Did you just come out here to harass me?*—but I kept it to myself.

The bell rang five minutes before I had to be back in class, which meant I was still early. I pushed my way through meandering kids to get to my classroom, but before I could make it there, a commotion started in front of me.

Someone—a teenage boy—had come out of the bathroom throwing up.

"Ewww, you're supposed to puke *inside* the bathroom," a girl said.

The boy heaved again.

A circle formed around him. I tried to get through to my classroom but was unsuccessful.

"What's the matter, dude?" Another boy patted the puking one on the back before walking toward the bathroom doors. "Did someone drop a stink bomb or something?"

Not twenty seconds after he walked into the bathroom, the boy came bursting out, his face white as a ghost. "D-dead. She-she's dead." Then he retched, too.

This was enough to set me into action. I'd been to enough crime scenes to know how things went. "Everyone get back."

A couple of teenagers laughed as if it were a joke. A few others took a step back.

"I'm serious," I said. "Take a step back, right now."

The slight movement allowed me to wedge myself through the group, over the growing puddle of vomit, and stand in front of the bathroom doors. "No one else is allowed inside this bathroom."

I pulled my phone from my pocket and called Jake.

"How's my favorite mayoral candidate?" Jake answered, his voice full of sunshine.

"Guarding a bathroom at the high school," I said.

"Why are you—"

"I think there's a dead body inside."

"You think? Or you know?" Through the receiver, I could hear Jake standing from his chair and grabbing the keys off his desk.

The hallway was silent as the teenagers listened to me, horror spreading across their faces.

"I haven't been inside yet, but two boys went in and came out vomiting."

"I'll be there right away," Jake said. "Do you think you can go inside and make sure someone isn't just hurt?"

"Sure," I said. "I can do that."

"See you soon," he said and hung up.

I took a deep breath, unsure of what I would find behind the bathroom door when I caught Nick's eye over the heads of the teenagers.

"You're late for class," he said. "That means you're out of the race."

"But—"

"No excuses, no exceptions."

"What about for a dead body?" I asked.

He laughed. "Oh right, like I'm going to believe—"

The growing murmurs of the teenagers cut off his statement.

"Did she say dead body?"

"Who died?"

"Someone was murdered."

"Shot."

"Gutted."

A scream pierced the air, and chaos broke out.

Teenagers plowed into each other, trying to get away from the bathroom.

The two boys doubled over, throwing up, were nearly trampled by their peers.

I stepped over to help them up, but before I could grab their arms, my foot slipped, and I fell hard on my back.

A warmth spread from my lower back up to my neck. I didn't need to smell it to know what it was.

All I could think was: *Which is worse—dog poop or vomit?*

8

I struggled to get back on my feet without getting more of the vomit on me. And without throwing up all over the place myself.

A hand jutted out at me. It was Nick's. He looked utterly unfazed by the vomit surrounding us and all over me.

"Do you want help up, or are you just going to slide around in the vomit all day?" Nick might have been doing a good thing by helping me up, but he wasn't exactly doing it in the kindest way.

I took his hand, and he practically lifted me to a stand.

"Thanks," I said.

"Why were they puking? And what's wrong with the bathroom? Did I hear you say someone died in there?"

The two boys who had been throwing up had disbursed with the rest of the kids, leaving Nick and me in the hallway alone.

"Stay out here for a second," I said. "I need to go in and see if whoever is in there might need help."

"I'm the mayor of this town. I think I have every right to go into the bathroom with you."

"I'm a police consultant," I said. "And Jake asked me specifically to go inside."

"Well, I'm going in with you."

"No, you're staying out here."

"Who will stop me? You?"

"I don't have time for this," I said. "Someone could be dying in there."

"Then, by all means, go inside." He motioned toward the door.

It was futile arguing with him. I needed to get in there.

I pulled the door open and walked inside.

At first glance, everything seemed normal. The sinks were straight in front of me, meaning the urinals and stalls were likely right around the corner opposite the sinks.

I took a breath and walked around the corner.

A woman—an adult woman—sat up against a closed bathroom stall. A handgun was on the floor a couple of inches from her right hand. From what I could tell, she hadn't been shot, as there was no blood around her.

But that didn't mean she was alive.

Her chin drooped down to her chest.

I pushed two fingers against her neck and found a dark red tie restricting her airway.

"Do you have a knife or anything I can cut this with?" I asked Nick. The tie was tied tight to the stall handle. I squatted in front of her and put my arms under hers. "I'll lift her so she can get air—if possible—while you cut her free."

Nick didn't reply. I lifted her dead weight, and though she wasn't probably any larger than me, she was still hard to hold up in a crouched position.

I couldn't hear her taking any breaths, but that was probably because of the sound of my own coming out in strained puffs.

"Nick, I need you to untie the tie." I glanced behind me to find the bathroom empty. He'd followed me inside —of that, I was certain. How had I missed the sound of him exiting?

I grumbled to myself, then lifted the woman as high as I could.

I slipped the looped tie around her face and over her head. When I did so, her head tipped back, revealing her identity.

Susan—Nick's ex-wife.

I lowered her to the ground and kneeled beside her to check for a pulse.

Nothing.

I tipped her head back and tried a few rescue breaths, but they wouldn't go in no matter how many times I repositioned her head.

With that, I started chest compressions. If the paramedics arrived quickly, they might be able to establish the airway. She couldn't have been like this for very long.

My knees ached against the tile floor as if they had shards of glass cutting into them with every motion, but I couldn't stop the compressions even after it felt like I'd been doing them for hours.

When Jake and the paramedics walked in, I was happy to give them control.

"We found her against the stall door with the tie—" I stood and pointed to the tie that was still looped around the handle of the closed stall. "—around her neck. I lifted her and got the loop around her head, then noticed who she was."

"Are you bleeding?" Jake asked, glancing down at my knees. "Your pants are ripped."

"How did that happen?" I inspected the holes in my pants and the cuts in my knees.

Jake picked up a shard of glass with his gloved hand. "I bet these shards are the culprits."

Apparently, it wasn't just a feeling that I had glass cutting my knees. I'd actually had glass cutting my knees.

"You said we," Jake said, slipping the shards of glass into a plastic evidence bag after placing a numbered marker on the floor. "Before, you said 'We found her.' What did you mean by that?"

"Nick insisted he come in with me, but he probably recognized Susan before I did and let himself out of the bathroom."

The paramedics had inserted a tube in Susan's throat and gotten her onto a gurney.

"What about the gun?" Jake asked.

"It was a few inches from her right hand, but I didn't see any blood or gunshot wounds on her."

"Did anyone hear any gunshots?"

I shrugged. "I'm guessing they didn't because what drew attention to the bathroom was the first kid who came out throwing up."

"Is that what's all over you?" Jake asked.

"I might have fallen," I said, remembering that I was covered in vomit.

The paramedics left with Susan on the stretcher.

"Do you think she'll be okay?" I asked.

"Only time will tell," Jake said. "What was tied around her neck?"

We walked closer to where she'd been hanging. "I think it's a necktie." It was then that it hit me. "I've seen this tie before. Deacon was wearing it."

"As in the other Mayor for a Day nominee?"

"He had it on in class this morning," I said. "Maybe he tried to kill her and make it look like a suicide."

"What's on it?" Jake used his gloved hand to lift the tie from where it hung and examine it. "It looks like green glitter."

"What?" I inched closer for a look. "Laura was using green glitter on her poster."

"Poster?" Jake asked.

"We had to make posters in class this morning. Coral —the event planner—practically took over the class. Laura made a big deal about using green glitter on her poster."

Jake looked confused.

"If she had green glitter on her—which I'm sure she did since glitter practically never goes away—maybe she had something to do with this."

"Like she helped Susan commit suicide?" Jake asked.

I shrugged. "Or maybe Susan used green glitter on her poster, too?"

"Seems a bit more plausible." Jake pushed on the stall door. "Why is this locked?"

I hadn't considered it would have to be locked for Susan to be propped up against it.

He used his pocketknife to turn the metal circle until the door swung open, revealing a gruesome scene.

Judging by the bullet holes in Deacon's chest, I'd venture to guess he'd died within minutes of being shot.

"Maybe we should check him for green glitter, too," I said.

9

"What do you think happened?" Jake asked me. "Any feelings about this one?"

I reached into my magic to search for any hints. Something felt off.

I touched the tie with a gloved hand and felt something buzzing back at me. "This tie—there's something here."

Jake waited and watched as I made my way around the bathroom. The gun was still on the floor with a little evidence marker next to it. I touched my pointer finger to the tip of the weapon, and a jolt nearly sent me backward.

"The gun and the tie—I think they belonged to someone with magic," I said.

Jake eyed me. "Haven't you learned to sense someone with magic? If the tie was on Deacon, maybe he was a warlock."

I shook my head. "I didn't sense it as him, but I could be wrong." I couldn't tell him I was rarely wrong about this. The town coroner—Neve—was a witch with a powerful masking spell, so other witches and warlocks couldn't sense she had magic. But I still could. Probably because I was next in line to be the Grand Witch.

"Is there anyone else who has magic around other than you and Xander?" Jake asked.

I thought of Andrea and the slight glow of magic around her. But she and Susan were best friends. She surely wouldn't have killed her best friend. And it wasn't my place to out her unless I thought she was indeed a threat.

"Maybe I should re-word that question," Jake said, noticing my hesitation. "I understand why you wouldn't want to tell me about someone who doesn't want to be outed as magical. So how about this? If you were to guess what happened here, what would you guess, and who would you look into?"

I thought about this for a moment. "If I had to guess, I wouldn't think there was anything strange about the situation. To me, it looks like Susan shot Deacon, then took his tie and hung herself."

"And if there *was* something strange about the situation?" Jake asked.

I sighed. "Then I'd look into the Mayor for a Day candidates and the mayor himself. He and Susan didn't seem to be on great terms."

Jake nodded once. "And what about Susan and Deacon? Did anything seem off about the two of them?"

"Nick accused them of having an affair," I said.

"I guess that means we should start with Nick."

I nodded, and Jake followed me down the deserted

hallway to the classroom we'd been in for the Mayor for a Day training.

Laura sat alone in the room, staring blankly at the whiteboard. When she heard our footsteps, she whipped around with a look of sheer terror on her face.

"Are you okay?" Jake asked, taking a step toward her.

"Nick said she's dead," Laura whispered. "Is that true? Is Susan dead?"

"Nick came in here?" I asked.

"Is Susan dead?" Laura asked again.

Jake glanced down at his phone and turned the screen toward me. A text message gave the bad news.

"I'm sorry, she didn't make it," Jake said. "Were the two of you close?"

"How did she die?" Laura asked.

"That's still under investigation," I said.

Jake gave me a proud look that made me feel all warm and gooey on the inside. So much so it almost could have changed the ebony hue of my hair. Unfortunately, finding two people dead was a strong feeling to combat.

"Did Nick say anything when he came in here other than tell you Susan was dead?" I asked.

Laura narrowed her eyes at me. "I don't need to answer your questions. You're not a cop."

"She's aiding me," Jake said, his voice kind and low.

We both had the same blue eyes and liked the crispy edges of our pancakes. Not that that meant anything in the grand scheme of things. But when I first moved to Cliff Haven, I thought it meant he was my father.

"He told me she was dead and that I should leave.

That it might not be safe," Laura said. "Then he picked up his stuff and ran out."

I glanced at Jake, who still had his focus on Laura.

"Wasn't there another candidate for the Mayor for a Day?" Jake asked.

"Two," Laura said. "Deacon and Andrea. Neither of them has come back from lunch. Deacon, Andrea, and Susan left together. Nick stayed in the room with Coral. And I went outside to speak with Ellie before coming back here. Nick and Coral were gone at that point."

She was speaking so quickly I was having a hard time piecing together the timeline. I tried to sum it up, "So, Coral told us we could go to lunch. After I left, Susan, Andrea, and Deacon left together."

Laura looked at me like I was the dumbest thing since square wheels.

"Did you see which way they went?" I asked.

She shook her head. "But I left not too long after them and didn't see them on my way out to talk to you."

"I don't think they followed me out," I said. "I was watching because Deacon was giving me the heebie-jeebies."

"And Nick and Coral were left alone in the room?" Jake asked.

"Yes," she said, exasperation in her tone. "They were cleaning up the craft supplies and hanging the posters." She motioned to where the posters hung to dry with their faces toward the wall.

"And they were gone when you returned after we spoke?" I asked.

"Yes," she said, exasperation changing into irritation.

"I came back here and ate my lunch alone."

I glanced down at the sandwich with only one bite out of it, and the container of grapes was still almost full. There were no other wrappers or containers of any kind, though maybe she'd discarded them or put them back in her bag.

"And then Nick came in, told me Susan was dead and that I should go, and ran out of the room," Laura said. "I've never seen him so agitated before. I mean, I know his ex-wife was just murdered, but still."

Why did Laura instantly think Susan had been murdered? "Did Nick say she was dead, or she'd been murdered?"

The corner of Jake's mouth twitched.

"What's the difference?" Laura asked.

"Can you think back to what his exact words were?" Jake asked, his voice calm. He and I were both thinking the same thing. If Laura had created the murdered idea in her own head without Nick saying it, she might be responsible.

"He said she was dead," Laura said. "I'm sorry. She probably wasn't murdered. I guess with everything that's gone on the past few months, I just assumed. I guess she could have killed herself."

"How would you think Susan might kill herself?" Jake asked.

Laura looked at him as if he'd just told her she was adopted. Which definitely wouldn't have been the same face I would have made if someone told me I was adopted. She looked utterly disgusted. "How would I know?"

"You knew Susan," Jake said. "Maybe you could

venture a guess?"

"Maybe with a gun," Laura said. "I don't know. It's too horrible to think about. How did she die? What happened?"

"Again, we can't discuss this right now," Jake said. "She and Andrea were good friends, right?"

Laura nodded. "Andrea will be devastated."

"What about Deacon? He went to lunch with them. Was he one of their friends too?" I asked. "Other than the whole alleged cheating thing?"

"It didn't seem like they were friends," Laura said. "All Deacon did was talk about you."

"Me?" I asked, taken aback.

"He wanted to know all about you," Laura said. "As they were walking out of the room for lunch, he asked one of them where you lived."

A shiver ran down my spine. Why had Deacon wanted to know about me?

My emotions were all over the place. Deacon was dead, so I couldn't exactly ask him these questions.

Footsteps entering the room interrupted my thoughts.

Xander walked in wearing a leather jacket, dark jeans, and a worried look on his face. "Are you okay? I heard what happened."

Tears flooded my eyes at the sight of him.

He opened his arms. I took a step toward him, but before I could get there, Laura pushed past me and fell into him. He embraced her tightly and pressed his face into his hair as she sobbed.

I felt like someone had knocked the wind out of me.

Jake grabbed my elbow to steady me.

Before I started crying in front of everyone, I walked out of the classroom, past the crime scene, and back onto the front lawn.

I slid down a large tree and put my head between my knees, letting the tears fall to the dirt. Everything was so overwhelming with the pressure to become the Grand Witch of the States, this Mayor for a Day business, and two dead bodies—one of which had been strangely interested in my personal life. Then nearly embarrassing the daylights out of myself by falling into an embrace meant for another woman.

What had I been thinking? Of course, he was reaching for Laura.

I hugged my knees closer, wishing I could simply turn myself into a tiny ball and disappear. My scalp tingled with an overwhelm of emotions. I could only imagine what colors my hair was changing.

Home.

Why couldn't I just be home?

In my bed?

With Penelope at my side.

A rush of air flooded my ears as if a tornado had dropped out of the sky and landed with me in the eye. But when I looked up, the world was fuzzy. So fuzzy, I couldn't make out where I was.

Was I about to pass out? I sucked in a deep breath and squeezed my eyes closed, trying to steady myself.

As I exhaled, I opened my eyes, and the deafening sound stopped.

The tingling in my scalp and the oink at my side confirmed what my eyes didn't want to believe.

10

"How did I get here?" I asked Penelope, but she looked just as confused as I was.

She snuggled up into my lap as I pulled the covers on my unmade bed over the both of us.

"Does this mean I can time travel?" I asked. "Or—uh—place travel? Magically?"

Penelope grunted quietly. I closed my eyes again and then opened them quickly.

We were still in my bedroom.

Just then, a buzzing came from the floor.

When I peeked over the side of my bed, I saw my backpack—it had traveled with me—and a frightened-looking Wix.

I picked up the backpack and dug the cell phone out.

"Hello?" I said, knowing it was Jake.

"What the heck just happened? Where are you? One minute you're hyperventilating against a tree, and the next, you're gone. It's like you disappeared." He laughed, but the laugh wasn't out of humor. It was the laugh he made when he found out something new about my magic.

"I'm at home," I said, rubbing Wix behind the ears. "I don't know how it happened, but I wanted to be home, and, when I opened my eyes, I was."

The line was silent.

"Jake?" I asked. "I'm just as freaked out as you are."

"You should probably call someone and talk to them about this whole disappearing thing. Someone magical."

I used to call Xander for my magical questions. But since he and Laura had become more serious, I'd tried to stay out of their way.

"I'll call Lucy and Renée," I said. "They'll know what to do."

"I have no idea," Lucy said. She and Renée sat in my living room with Wix snuggled between them on the sofa. Penelope and I were curled up in the oversized chair with a large fluffy blanket.

While I waited for Renée and Lucy to arrive, I'd taken a shower and thrown my sheets into the washer to get the vomit off. Now, I had both the smell of dog poop and vomit lodged in my nostrils.

"You have no idea?" I turned to Renée. "And you?"

"Sorry, I don't either," Renée said. "Are you certain you didn't pass out, and someone brought you home and tucked you into bed?"

The two women in front of me were some of the smartest and kindest I'd ever met. There hadn't been a question—magical or not—they couldn't answer between the two of them. Until now.

"No one brought me home," I said. "Jake saw me disappear. And I wasn't tucked in bed. I was sitting on top of it."

"So, you think you traveled magically through time and space because of your emotions?" Renée asked. "And how did Mona get here?"

"Mona's here?" I asked.

"She's parked in the garage," Lucy said. "Maybe you got inside, and she drove you home?"

I shook my head and stood, leaving Penelope asleep on the chair. "I didn't come home in Mona. She must have brought herself home."

"She can't just bring herself home," Lucy said. "We've discussed this. Mona only has magic through your magic."

I wasn't about to argue the details about this with her. She and I had agreed to disagree that Mona did, in fact, have her own magic.

"I was upset—really upset—more upset than I've been in a long time," I said.

"Because Xander embraced Laura," Renée said.

"And all the other things I mentioned." I sighed. It wasn't just because of Xander.

"But mostly because of Xander, right?" Lucy asked. "I mean, you've never gotten this worked up over a dead body before. And could you stop pacing, please? You're making me dizzy."

"Does it matter why I was upset?" I stopped pacing and crossed my arms over my chest. "I just was."

"Matters of the heart can have a significant effect on

our magical abilities. Love has been known to make witches and warlocks incredibly powerful," Renée said.

"But it can also make them lose their powers, too," Lucy said.

"That's true," Renée said.

"I'm not in love with Xander," I said. "He's a friend. I'm seeing his cousin."

"Seeing him when?" Renée asked. "Months ago?"

"We have a long-distance understanding." The understanding was we hung out if we ended up in the other person's country. Otherwise, all bets were off. But I wasn't about to tell Lucy and Renée this.

"Just because you're dating one man—long distance—doesn't mean you can't have feelings for another," Lucy said, her tone gentle. "It's okay if you love him."

I started pacing again. The movement helped me think. "I don't. This wasn't about love. If anything, it was about pride. I almost embarrassed myself. If I'd have fallen into Xander's arms, it would have been terrible. Laura might have killed me on the spot."

"Laura may hate you, but she's no murderer," Renée said.

"How do you know?" I asked. "She said she ate her lunch, but it was almost completely untouched, and what about the green glitter?"

"Not eating one's lunch hardly means they're a murderer," Renée said.

"But green glitter does." Lucy giggled.

"That's not what I was—it doesn't matter. What I'm saying is—I was overwhelmed with everything. The potential embarrassment I'd dodged must have put me over the edge. My scalp was tingling like my arm does when I fall asleep on it wrong. It was almost painful. And then the whirlwind of air. And then I was here. On my bed. With Penelope."

Penelope still slept soundly on the chair.

"It had to be my magic," I said.

"Yes," Renée said. "I think we all agree it was your magic. It's just not magic I've ever seen before."

"Do you think you could do it again?" Lucy asked.

"Maybe," I said. "Though I'd rather not go back into hysterics. I try my best to stay level-headed."

"I don't see there being another way to recreate it," Renée said. "But let's try another day. If I had to guess, your magic is likely drained at the moment."

Come to think of it, I was rather tired.

"Why don't you try something simple," Lucy said. "Light the candles on the mantle."

This was one of the first things Lucy had taught me to do magically. Now, I could do it from a completely different room. I'd only charred the wallpaper a couple of times.

But when I tried, nothing happened. Just the attempt made me feel like I might pass out with exhaustion.

"That's what I thought," Lucy said. "You need some hearty food and rest."

"I'll get to cooking," Renée said, standing.

"No," both Lucy and I practically shouted.

Renée giggled. "I was kidding."

Renée was a terrible cook—even worse than me. She couldn't make pasta without burning the water or popcorn without infesting the house with black smoke.

"I'll whip something up," Lucy said, standing. "You need to sit back down. Better yet, why don't you head up to bed? I'll bring dinner up when it's ready."

Renée, Penelope, and I started toward the stairs when the doorbell rang.

I turned and opened the door.

"Hello, Ellie Vanderwick," Harriet—my cousin—said. "It is nice to see you again."

I couldn't help the excitement bubbling in my chest. I pulled Harriet into a massive hug. She stood stiff as a board, waiting for it to be over.

"Where did you go? Why did you leave in such a hurry? I'm so glad you're—"

Before I could finish my statement, the world went black.

11

I woke up in my freshly made bed. "Did I teleport here?" I asked Lucy and Renée, who were standing over me, waiting for me to wake up.

"No," Lucy said. "We brought you up."

"Where is Harriet?" I asked.

"She's in her room with Wix," Renée said. "I asked her not to get you all worked up until you had time to recuperate from your day."

"But I need to talk to her." I started to sit up in bed, but Renée pushed me back with more strength than a woman of her age would usually have.

"I see you've still been doing the workouts I assigned you," I said with a chuckle.

"Every day." Renée beamed. "You'll have plenty of time to catch up with Harriet in the morning. She's promised me she won't be leaving so suddenly this time."

"Does she know you're the Grand Witch?" I asked.

"I may have made that point known," Renée said.

Lucy snickered. "She definitely made it known."

"You don't have to worry about her leaving," Renée said. "I have to be going, but if you need anything, you can call Lucy or me or Xander."

"I will not be calling Xander," I said.

"He's still your—" Lucy started.

"Friend," Renée interrupted. "He's still your friend. And a warlock, to boot. Which means he's obligated to help you."

"Magical folks are obligated to help each other?" This was the first I heard of such a law.

"They are obligated to help the future Grand Witch of the States," Renée corrected.

"But what if I decided not to—"

"Do you want people to be obligated to help you or not?" Renée asked.

"I don't want Xander to be obligated to help me. I want him to want to help me."

Renée softened. "I know. And since he's your friend, I'm sure he wants to help you. So call him if you need to."

"What about Harriet?" I asked. "Wouldn't it be smarter for me to ask her if I needed something?"

"At this point, no," Renée said. "Harriet is unreliable at best. Until we can gauge her true motives, it's best not to divulge much to her or ask for help that may put you in her debt."

"But she's my cousin," I said. "I'm the future Grand Witch."

"Are you?" Lucy asked, quirking an eyebrow up at me.

I shrugged. "As far as everyone knows, I am."

Renée sighed. "We'll see you in the morning."

She and Lucy left Penelope and me alone in what used

to be my grandmother's room with a plateful of delicious-looking, likely magically prepared, food.

———

With my stomach full, my energy seemed to be returning. At least enough for me to go up to the attic to write down what was going on.

My grandmother's attic was magical and cozy and felt like a warm hug. Penelope followed me up the curved wooden staircase. She gazed out the window toward the magical pond as I folded myself into the oversized leather chair.

The journal was still a mystery to me. It had been Esme's. She'd written in it nearly every day from the looks of things. However, some days I still couldn't understand the writing. It only transformed into something readable when it wanted me to read it.

Today, though, I had no intentions of reading. I needed to get my thoughts down before I forgot anything.

I started writing frantically on a new page—the energy coming directly from my full stomach. I wrote about the problems with Xander and my feelings for him, the bodies, my almost-embarrassment, and magically traveling through time and space.

My hand ached when I set the pen on the small table next to my chair. I reread what I'd written, and when I was satisfied, I let out a deep exhale.

Penelope oinked quietly, and when I looked up at her, I realized she wasn't alone.

I nearly screamed at the sight of my grandmother—my

dead grandmother—sitting next to Penelope and staring out the window. Esme shimmered in an unearthly manner —similarly to how she had in a dream I'd had not too long ago.

She was a ghost. And that dream probably hadn't been a dream.

Once I got over my shock, I admired the sight before me. Penelope had a slight lean to her body—one I might not have noticed—as she leaned against Esme. Esme rubbed behind Penelope's ears, and Penelope seemed to respond in muted grunts and oinks.

I couldn't hear Esme saying anything, though.

Xander told me ghosts existed, but I hadn't believed him.

Now, I knew they did. And Penelope could see them. I glanced around. How many other ghosts had she been able to see?

I couldn't see any.

"Ah, it looks like she's done," Esme said to Penelope. "Now, to show her a bit about what happened."

The journal in my lap flipped to a few pages in the front. It had done this before—turned to a page it wanted me to read—but I'd thought the journal itself was magical, not that my ghostly grandmother was controlling it.

"What?" I acted like I didn't know what was happening, and Esme giggled a little. I did my best not to smile at the glorious sound.

Penelope oinked and walked to my feet as I read.

It happened again today. I teleported. My emotions took over and I wished I was home. And in an instant, I was.

I've never teleported anywhere but here, so maybe it's the house. Maybe I put too much magic in it. Maybe it can call me back when I need it to.

I'm not certain.

This time I knew what was happening before it did. The whooshing sound of the wind in my ears alerted my mind to the terrifying first experience. But this time wasn't so bad. And maybe if I can learn to control it, I'll be able to travel to other places too.

I closed the journal and looked up. Esme's ghost was gone.

As I was finishing breakfast the next morning, Harriet and Wix came meandering down the stairs.

"Coffee?" she asked.

I poured her a cup just like she liked it—black.

"Thanks." She took a sip and nodded in approval.

"So?" I asked.

"So what?"

"Where did you go? Why did you leave without saying goodbye?"

"My time here was done," she said. "I had to move on with the investigation."

"Xander told you to leave, didn't he?" I asked.

"How are you and Xander?"

"He's dating someone else. And I'm dating his cousin from Argentina."

"Long distance never works." Her voice was monotone and matter-of-fact, as always. She reached down and patted Wix on the head. He'd barely left her side since she arrived.

"You haven't answered my question."

"Does it matter why I left? I'm here now."

"Are you going to do another disappearing act?" My hands were shaking so badly because of the confrontation with my only known living relative that I had to set my coffee down on the counter.

"I told you last night, I'll be here a while."

"How long is a while?"

"Long enough," she said.

"Did you solve your mystery?"

She didn't look up from her coffee. The reason she'd come to Cliff Haven in the first place was because she thought someone was out to kill her—the same person or family who had killed her mother and grandmother.

"It's not important anymore."

"And why is that?" I asked.

"Because Monroe isn't trying to kill us anymore."

"Who is Monroe?"

"Our cousin," she said. "The one who was trying to kill us, remember?"

"You never told me his name," I said. "Why has he decided not to kill us?"

She looked up from her coffee and gave me an exasperated sigh. "No one would be stupid enough to kill the next Grand Witch of the States."

"But I was in line to be the next one when you came before."

"You didn't know that," Harriet said.

"I would have found out, eventually."

"Maybe." She shrugged. "Or maybe not. If he'd have killed you before you found out, it could have been a loophole."

"Pretty sure murder is murder, any way you slice it."

"Not when it comes to the Grand Witch."

"Then how does this relate to you?"

"If he's not going to kill you, there would be no reason to kill me."

"Unless he wants half of what's owed to him rather than a third."

She shook her head. "You are ridiculous. You know that?"

"How?"

"You don't know anything."

"Then enlighten me." I glanced at my phone screen. "And quickly because I need to get to my Mayor for a Day class."

"Being the next Grand Witch of the States means you'll get all the inheritance."

I thought about that for a minute. "Is that the only reason you're here? You wanted to get back in my good graces?" My voice was softer than I wanted it to be. Fragile. If the only reason she was back was to suck up to me, I didn't want to know. But I needed to know.

"I'm back because there's no danger anymore," she said. "And I thought it would be nice to be closer to my only remaining family member."

Even though she sounded less than pleased, my heart swelled with joy.

"I'm glad you came back. Dewdrop is always open for you." Each of the rooms in my house had a name and chose who they allowed to sleep in them. Harriet's room was Dewdrop.

She smiled. "Now, tell me more about this Mayor for a Day thing."

I left Harriet, Wix, and Penelope at the house with strict instructions to take care of one another and not get into any trouble. Harriet promised me she'd make sure Wix got his exercise so he wouldn't destroy my brand new throw pillows.

Mona happily rumbled down the dirt road toward the main highway that led to town.

"How are you, Mona?" I asked. "Did you have a nice drive without me yesterday?"

The steering wheel warmed beneath my hands.

I'd recently learned Mona could use her own mind to do things—such as drive super fast and go after people she didn't like.

But I couldn't have her out there driving around by herself. No one needed to know my van had a mind of her own.

"You can't just drive around without me," I said. "Even if you know—wait—did you know I'd teleported?"

The steering wheel warmed again.

"Well, don't do it again if you can help it." Maybe I'd somehow willed her to follow me.

The location for the second day of classes had been changed last-minute to the library community room.

When I walked in, Laura sat at the desk talking to a

couple of children and their mothers. She looked so kind at that moment, I almost didn't recognize her.

Her demeanor changed the instant the mothers and children walked past me out the door, and her gaze landed on me. "The room's back there." She pointed to the other side of the library.

"Thanks," I said, then took a deep breath. If she and Xander were going to be together, I needed to get to know her better. Especially if I wanted to keep Xander as a friend. "You seem to enjoy your job."

"What's not to enjoy about books? They're just about the best thing in the entire world."

I could think of a few things that were better—double fudge ice cream with sprinkles being one—but I wasn't about to contradict her. "Do you have a favorite?"

She gaped at me. "Why do people always ask if I have a favorite book? That would be like choosing between my children, I mean, if I had any. It's impossible. They all have their pros and cons. Even the terrible ones. Every book is a work of art, just like a painting."

I'd never thought of books that way. To me, books had simply been a way to get through school and occasionally pass the time. Like when I'd broken my leg snowboarding and wasn't able to do much physical activity.

"We should get to class," she said. "Don't want to get kicked out on day two."

"Or killed," I said, then instantly regretted it. "I'm sorry, that was terrible."

Laura giggled. "Actually, it was slightly funny. Too soon, of course, but funny still."

It might have been funny to think the Mayor for a Day

class had anything to do with the possibility of being murdered, but those two people were someone's family members, and here I was making a joke about their deaths. That wasn't funny at all.

Laura walked in first and took a seat near the front of the class. I wasn't feeling terribly outgoing today, so I took one in the second row.

Nick stood with his back to us, trying to get a projector to work. Andrea was the only other person in the room. She wore another pantsuit. This time, it was a dark blue, and her hair was twisted into a neat bun on top of her head. Her magic glistened around her faintly. Could she have been the one responsible for Susan and Deacon's deaths?

When Nick turned around, he looked like he'd been up all night. "Today." His voice was scratchy. He cleared his throat and started over. "Today, we're going to talk about the inner workings of being a Mayor."

That was it? We weren't going to discuss what had happened the day before? Or why there were two empty chairs in the room?

"Wait," Laura said. "We still have a couple of minutes, and Deacon's not here."

I glanced around. Did she not know Deacon had been killed too?

"Correct," Nick said. "Forgive me. I'll wait until he's officially late. But I doubt he'll be showing up."

"Why is that?" Laura asked.

"Because I spent all night trying to find him." Nick shoved a hand through his hair.

"Why would you be looking for Deacon?" Laura asked, her voice less confident with this question.

"Because he killed Susan."

Laura gasped.

Andrea looked up with wide eyes.

No one in this room knew that Deacon had been in that bathroom, too. That it looked like Susan had killed him.

"From what I heard, she did it to herself," Laura said.

"I was there. I saw her," Nick said. "Susan didn't do that. Wouldn't do that."

"It does seem strange that she would come to class if she was just planning to end it all in the middle of the day," Laura said.

"Why do you think someone killed her?" I asked Nick. "Because when I was in the bathroom, my first impression was that she'd died by suicide."

"Didn't you see the gun?" Nick asked.

"Yes, but she wasn't shot," I said.

"Maybe someone held her at gunpoint and forced her to do that," Nick said. "Someone who had been wearing a red tie."

Laura gasped. "She used Deacon's tie?"

"Why do you think I've been looking for him?" Nick asked. "She might have been my ex-wife, but I still cared about her."

Andrea guffawed.

"What?" Nick turned his attention to his old rival. "I did."

"Didn't you go to lunch with Deacon and Susan?" I asked Andrea. "Did anything seem off with them?"

"We walked out of the room together, but we didn't go to lunch together. Deacon had to use the bathroom, so Susan and I took a walk down memory lane," Andrea said, a tear in her eye. "Then I got a phone call and excused myself. I told her I'd meet them back in the classroom."

"But you never came back," Laura said.

"When I came back, the classroom was empty. I waited, but no one came," Andrea said. "I figured Nick had let us out early, so I went home."

"You must have come after Xander and I left," Laura said.

"I didn't know Susan was dead until I came to class this morning." She wiped a tear from her face.

"Deacon's time is up," Nick said and turned to the whiteboard to start writing.

I pulled my phone out of my backpack and typed out a message to Jake about what Andrea said.

Jake's message came back quickly.

Do you think Andrea did it?

I replied:

> *I think it's possible. But I wouldn't count Nick or even Laura out at this point.*

Laura? You're not letting your personal life intrude on your professional duties, right?

I scoffed.

No. She didn't eat her lunch like she said she did. She was the one with the green glitter. And she said Susan was murdered. Not dead. Murdered. Like she knew.

I highly doubt Laura is to blame for this.

I rolled my eyes, even though I knew he was probably right.

Can I tell the class that Deacon is dead?

"Is there something more pressing in your lap than learning about becoming mayor?" Nick asked.

My head shot up. "Uh, no. Sorry." I felt my phone vibrate again.

"Put your phone away, or I will confiscate it."

I almost laughed. He couldn't take my phone. But he could kick me out of the class. At this point, trash cans seemed like a stupid reason to put up with Nick's crap.

I looked down to slip the phone back into my pocket but checked Jake's reply first.

The family's been notified. Soon the whole town will know. You can tell them but no details. Keep an eye out for suspicious behavior. And whatever you do, don't get kicked out of that class. One of those people might be the murderer.

I must have lingered slightly too long reading Jake's text because Nick strode to my desk and held his hand out. "Give it to me."

"I—uh—it was Jake," I said. "He wanted me to let you know Deacon is dead."

Andrea and Laura both whipped around to look at me.

Nick narrowed his eyes. "Let me see the text."

"No," I said, almost laughing at the thought of him looking through my text messages. "It's private."

"How can I know you were on official business without you showing me?" Nick still held his hand out in front of me.

"You can call Jake and ask him," I said. "But I'm not letting you look at my text messages."

"Fine, I'll call him when we break for lunch," Nick said. "Now, hand me the phone."

I hesitated.

"Hand me the phone or get out of my classroom."

Jake told me to stay in the class. I clicked my phone off so Nick would have to know the password to get in, then handed it to him.

"You'll get this back at the end of the day."

He slid it into his pocket and continued his lecture.

"Wait," Laura said. "Can we go back to Deacon being dead for a minute?"

Nick let out a frustrated sigh. "It serves him right after what he did."

"What did he do?" I asked.

"He killed Susan," Nick said. "He strangled her with his tie!"

"If he killed Susan, and he ended up dead after you were out looking for him all night, don't you think that makes you their prime suspect?" Andrea asked.

"That's ridiculous," Nick said. "I didn't actually find him."

"How do we know that?" Andrea asked. "Maybe you thought as mayor you had some strange duty to keep the town safe, so you took matters into your own hands."

"It is my job to keep the town safe," Nick said. "Through the first responders."

"If you didn't kill him, who did?" Andrea asked.

"How would I know?" Nick said, then turned to me. "How did he die?"

"I'm not of liberty to discuss the case," I said.

Laura was being really quiet. And she looked nervous, twisting her hands in her lap.

"Deacon's platform was to lower taxes," Andrea said. "Maybe someone wasn't happy about taking a pay cut."

"It wouldn't have come out of my paycheck," Nick said.

"Or maybe it's because of Susan and Deacon's affair," Laura said, almost in a whisper.

Nick signed. "She was my ex-wife. Ex. Which meant she was free to be with whomever she chose."

Laura didn't reply.

Nick glanced around the room, but no one said anything else. "If that's all the speculation, we should get on with our lesson."

By lunch, all I'd learned was that Nick had a massive stick up his butt and that Laura and Andrea seemed just as uninterested in the inner workings of being a mayor as I was.

Instead of leaving the classroom to eat, I stayed inside, figuring it was probably the safest place to be.

Laura and Andrea did the same.

As Nick was about to walk out the door, I said, "Can I have my phone back, please?"

He reluctantly pulled it from his pocket and handed it to me. "I'll want it back when class starts again."

I didn't reply. It was no use fighting with him.

When I checked the screen, I had thirty-nine text messages. All from Jake.

I hadn't even unlocked my phone when Jake came bursting through the doors, nearly knocking Nick out on his way in.

"Oh, thank goodness," he said. "Why haven't you been answering my texts?"

"Nick took my phone," I said.

Jake turned his gaze on Nick. "You took her phone?"

Nick puffed up his chest. "It was a distraction to the class."

"This class is supposed to be part of a fun tradition, not a boot camp," Jake said.

"My class, my rules." Nick wasn't backing down. "If she doesn't like it, she can drop out of the Mayor for a Day race."

"Technically, she needs that phone to help me with this investigation," Jake said. "And by taking it, I could charge you for impeding an investigation."

"That seems a bit of a stretch," Nick said.

"It's not a stretch at all," Jake said, his tone serious. "And I'm not above arresting the mayor."

Nick looked like Jake had just slapped him across the face.

"None of us are above the law," Jake continued. "In fact, we must be the poster children for the law. Now, you won't be taking anyone's phones during this class. Do you understand?"

"But they have nothing to do with the investigation," Nick said.

"They're adults," Jake said. "And if they're not paying attention in your class, they will fail the tests and be kicked out."

I'd almost forgotten about the tests. I hadn't been taking notes all morning. I was definitely going to get kicked out.

"I need to speak with Ellie, if you don't mind," Jake said.

"We're on lunch," Nick said.

He pushed past Jake and out the doors.

Jake and I walked out into the library, leaving Laura and Andrea in the community room together.

"What's going on?" I asked.

"Neve has been working all night on this. You know the glass that cut your knees?"

"Yeah," I said.

"It's glass from a camera lens," Jake said. "Also, Neve realized Susan didn't die by strangulation. She died of suffocation."

"Isn't that the same thing?" I asked.

"They both do the same thing, but she was dead before

whoever suffocated her put that tie around her neck to make it look like a suicide."

"Did she shoot Deacon?"

Jake glanced around. "No. There was no gunshot residue on either of her hands or anywhere near her, but the gun next to her was the gun that shot Deacon. Plus, she had to have been dead before he was shot."

"So, someone set them up to make it look like a murder-suicide," I said. "But who? And why?"

"Has anyone acted strangely in class today?"

"Everyone," I said. "Andrea tried to throw Nick under the bus for killing Susan. Then Laura jumped on board. She said Deacon and Susan were having an affair. Nick is being more insane than yesterday—taking phones and such. But I think he was up all night. He said he was looking for Deacon because he thought Deacon killed Susan."

"That's still a possibility," Jake said.

"Do you think Deacon could have shot himself?"

"No," Jake said. "There were too many gunshots wounds."

"So maybe he killed Susan, and then someone else killed him?"

"It's possible," Jake said. "Or someone killed them both."

"Who is the gun registered to?" I asked.

"It's untraceable so far," Jake said. "The serial number's been filed off, and the bullets don't match up to anything we can find in the system."

That was a dead end. I thought for a moment. "They all seemed surprised when I told them Deacon was dead."

"How surprised?"

"A realistic amount of surprised," I said. "But who knows?"

"Any more feelings?" Jake asked, glancing up at my hair.

Now that he mentioned it, I'd had no tingles in my scalp all day. "My magic was drained from the disappearing act yesterday. Maybe it hasn't come back yet."

"Well, when it does, you tell it we need its help," Jake said with a smile.

"How's Georgia?" I asked. Georgia was his fiancée and Xander's cousin.

"She's good," Jake said with a boyish grin. "We're in the throes of wedding planning, but she's great about it all. I even get to help decide some things."

"When's the big date?" I asked. I wasn't sure I'd be invited, though I hoped I would be.

"We haven't set one yet," Jake said. "But when we do, you'll be the first to know. I can't get married without my faux-daughter there."

My heart swelled with love. "I'm glad I'll be invited. I could understand why I wouldn't be."

"Nonsense," Jake said. "Georgia loves you."

I raised my eyebrows at him.

"Well, she definitely likes you," he said. "And she knows how important our relationship is to me."

"Me too," I said. "Now, let's figure out who killed Susan and Deacon."

Jake gave me strict orders to do well in the class and keep my eyes peeled.

When lunch was over, Nick walked back in with Coral.

"Coral is taking over for the rest of the day." Nick stood a few feet away from her as if she might lunge at him at any moment.

"Today, we'll begin the media part of the process," Coral said. "We'll work on your news interviews and your Instagram accounts."

I hated social media. Probably because I didn't have many friends to keep up with on the platform.

"If you already have a profile, you can update it to be your mayoral profile so you can keep your current followers."

Laura smirked at me. She had a massive following because of all the fun things she did for the town. It would be hard to keep up with her on that front.

"Is social media really that important?" Andrea asked.

"It seems stupid when I know everyone in this town. I ran an almost-successful campaign without social media."

"Let's just say, if you'd have had social media, you might be the one in Nick's shoes right now," Coral said with a hint of condescension in her voice.

Andrea huffed but didn't reply.

"If you would all pack up your belongings and follow me." Coral turned and started out the doors, then looked back and said, "Are we missing someone?"

"Oh," Nick said. "I figured you'd heard."

"Heard what?" Coral asked.

"Susan and Deacon died yesterday," he said. "Ellie's helping with the investigation."

"They died? Investigation?" She pulled out her phone and started texting furiously. "You have to tell me when things like this happen so I can deal with the media before they twist it into something unfavorable for the event."

I could feel irritation rising up my neck and into my scalp.

"Whoa," Nick said. "I knew you were a witch, but I guess it's different when you see it in person."

"What is that supposed to mean?" Coral whipped around, then noticed my hair. "Ah, right. You were talking about Ellie."

"You're a witch too?" Laura asked.

"That I am," Coral said. "But my hair doesn't change colors like a chameleon."

I pulled a strand of my typically white hair over my shoulder to find it was bright red. Usually, when it was red, that meant danger was close, or I was really mad.

I wasn't irritated enough with Coral's complete lack of

care for two of the candidates dying, which meant Jake must have been right about someone being dangerous, and possibly a killer.

"Let's try to keep the hair changing to a minimum, shall we?" Coral said. "It may seem like an advantage, but —trust me—magic will only ruin your campaign."

She seemed like she might have personal experience in the matter.

Coral marched out of the library like a woman on a mission. Laura and Andrea followed closely behind her, talking in whispers.

"Watch out for her," Nick said behind me.

I turned to look at him. "What do you mean?"

"She's part of the family who bought the strawberry farm. They've been known to make their gobs of money in any way possible. If you mess this up, she'll mess you up."

"As in kill me?"

He shrugged. "I just don't want you to get hurt."

Since when did he care about me?

"I mean any of you," he said. "No one. I don't want anyone—anyone else—to get hurt. Not just you. I couldn't care less about you. Just keep your eyes open."

I almost laughed. "Thanks for the warning."

I turned before he could say anything else.

My hair was still red, but as I walked out of the library, the tingles in my scalp faded. Did that mean Nick was the killer? He was the only one left in the library. Or maybe it had been Coral. She'd been there after all.

The tingling was so strange—so hard to figure out.

I still didn't know how Esme had been so in touch with her magic that she could help the police with cases.

I'd helped a few times, but those all felt random. Like I just stumbled upon a clue, and my magic made it more apparent. And just because I could tell that the gun and the tie had been around someone magical wasn't exactly the clarity I was looking for.

If only my magic could tell me more. Like who the killer was. Or—even better—when someone was thinking about killing so I could prevent it.

"Do you ever think about moving out of a town where so many murders occur?" Coral asked when we stopped in the middle of the square.

Laura shrugged. "Not really. This is my home. I wouldn't know where else to live."

Coral looked at Andrea.

"Same answer here," Andrea said. "I've lived here my whole life. Cliff Haven is the sweetest town in the world. It's just had some bad luck."

Coral turned her focus to me. "And how about you? You only just moved here. Would you consider leaving due to the dangerous atmosphere?"

I'd never thought of Cliff Haven as dangerous. "Maybe when I came across my first body," I said. "But I've since settled in. My grandmother's house is now mine, and I plan to hand it down to my own kids someday."

"Right," Coral said. "And how long do you think it'll be before you have children?"

"Uh," I said. "I don't know. I'm not married or anything."

"Do you have a boyfriend?" Coral asked.

"Kind of, I guess," I said.

"And where does he live?"

"In Argentina."

"And have you ever considered leaving Cliff Haven to be with him?"

Honestly, I hadn't. But I didn't know that this was any of her business. "I'm sorry," I said. "We only just met. Why is my personal life of interest?"

"I wondered when you'd push back." Coral smiled. "I was giving you a taste of what the reporters will ask. Every time you say something, you either give them a new grip to climb the mountain of information or leave them on their ledge. I'd suggest you lead them up the mountain in the direction you want them to go. Stay away from overhangs, danger zones, etcetera."

"What are you talking about?" Andrea asked.

"Climbing," I said. "She's talking about rock climbing. When you climb a mountain, you can take a variety of different paths depending on the hand and foot holds."

"Exactly," Coral said. "And those reporters want to climb your mountain of information in the most salacious way possible. Their goal is to drag out the dirt and get into your caves."

"Sounds dirty," Andrea said.

Laura smacked her and giggled.

"It'll get really dirty if they find out about any secrets. You think you're safe because you've been through the wringer once before when you went up against Nick, but you don't know what you're dealing with when we bring in the big guns."

"The big guns?" Laura asked with a gulp.

"City reporters," Coral said. "It's the only way we'll

make the Strawberry Festival a success. We have to get media coverage to get people to come."

"But if we're just boring old lumps, why would they want to come see us?" Laura asked.

Coral patted her on the shoulder. "That's why I'm here—to make sure you're not just boring old lumps."

Coral interviewed us repeatedly until we figured out our speeches and could answer just about any question she threw at us. It was refreshing, if not slightly exhausting, to learn a new skill.

When I got home, I found Penelope, Wix, and Harriet watching a serial killer documentary on the TV. Penelope looked genuinely frightened while Wix and Harriet were practically glued to the screen.

"You guys doing okay?" I asked.

Penelope squealed and dove under the blankets. Wix jumped off the couch and growled at me.

However, Harriet didn't seem the slightest bit surprised I was home. "Dinner's on the counter," she said before turning back to the TV.

I hadn't realized it had gotten so late. Since the time had changed, the days were getting longer and longer. It would explain the rumbling in my stomach.

Wix—realizing it was me—went back to the couch

with Harriet while Penelope followed me so closely, I almost tripped on her getting to the kitchen.

Dinner consisted of a half-eaten tub of microwaved leftover spaghetti I'd made three nights ago. I pulled out a clean fork and ate it standing at the kitchen sink.

The sunset painted the sky a pastel pink reflecting in the magical pond. I could just imagine swimming in the pond this summer. Over the winter, I'd had a strange occurrence where I'd ended up trapped in the ice. But since then, I'd honed my magical abilities slightly.

Which reminded me I needed to reschedule my lesson with Lucy.

I pulled my phone from my pocket and dialed her number.

"Is everything okay?" Lucy asked without even saying hello.

"Everything's fine," I said. "Great, even. My magic seems to be coming back."

"That was quick."

"Over twenty-four hours is quick?"

"After doing something no witch this side of history has done? I'd say you're lucky you got your magic back at all."

I took a bite of the spaghetti and immediately spit it back out. There was so much salt on it I felt like I'd just downed a bottle of soy sauce.

"I didn't realize I could lose my magic altogether." I took a drink of water. "Does that happen?"

"Not usually," Lucy said. "But you never know."

"Do you have time this week to fit me in for another lesson since I had to cancel?" I asked. "Now that my magic's back, I'd like to keep working on it." If anyone knew the importance of stretching your abilities, it was me.

"Do you have dinner plans?" she asked.

I glanced down at the spaghetti. "Nope."

"Good," she said. "Come on over and bring your cousin. She'll like it here."

When we pulled up to Lucy's tiny home, I glanced over to see Harriet's reaction. "It's not as small as it seems on the outside."

"You think I've never been to a magical town before?"

"I suppose you probably have," I said. "Sorry."

"I grew up in a house just like the one next door."

The house next door was the opposite of Lucy's. They were both tiny houses, but Lucy's was a five-story house that looked like a toddler had stacked their colorful blocks haphazardly atop one another. The one next door was a single-story painted bright white with light blue trim and a cute little fence around it.

"Did you like growing up in a magical town?" I asked.

"I didn't know any different." Harriet opened her door. "Are we going to sit out here and talk, or are we going inside?"

She was as salty as her spaghetti because I'd made her leave her documentary binge-watch to come to Lucy's for dinner after she'd already eaten.

Secretly, I thought she might have been sad to leave

Wix. But Wix wasn't trained well enough to take to other people's houses.

"Oh good, you're here," Lucy said when she opened the door. "Come in. Have a seat."

The inside was just as wacky as the outside, only more spacious. I sat where I usually did, in the oversized zebra print chair.

Harriet took the wooden rocking chair but sat on the edge with her feet firmly planted so the chair didn't have a chance of rocking back on her.

"I have soup and muffins," Lucy said. "How much would each of you like?"

"I'm not hungry," Harriet said. "But thanks."

"I'll have a full bowl," I said. "And a muffin. Do you need any help?"

"Not at all," Lucy said, making her way around the corner and into the kitchen. "Did you see the house for sale next door?"

"For sale?" Harriet perked up at the mention of this. "The white one?"

"That's the one," Lucy said. "The family moved out about a month ago and haven't found a suitable buyer."

Harriet turned to me. "Much like the rooms in your house, magical houses choose their buyer, not the other way around."

"What if someone insists on buying the wrong house?" I asked.

"The house will make them miserable." Harriet cracked a small smile. "I've heard some horror stories."

I could only imagine. Thankfully, my house only made

the beds uncomfortable if you were in the wrong room. At least, that had been my experience.

Lucy appeared with my food and an extra muffin, which she sat on the table next to Harriet. "In case you change your mind."

"Do you know how much they want for the house?" Harriet asked.

"I think for the right buyer, they'd do just about anything," Lucy said. "Why? Do you know someone in the market?"

Harriet looked down, fumbling with the zipper on her jacket. "Maybe."

"You just let me know. I'd be happy to show them around," Lucy said. "The owners have given me the authority to do so."

Harriet's head shot up. "Really?"

Lucy smiled. "Do you want to go look at it?"

Harriet nodded. "If it's not too much trouble."

"It's no trouble at all," Lucy said, then turned to me. "Would you like to come with us or stay and finish your food, dear?"

I gulped down the last bit of soup. "I'll come with."

Lucy laughed. "Were you hungry?"

"Starving," I said. "It was delicious. I'd ask for the recipe, but we all know I'd end up botching it somehow."

"It's magical soup," Lucy said. "Which makes it even harder to create."

"Then I'd surely do something wrong." I followed the other two out of the house, down the walk, through the gate, and to the other house.

"This house comes with a state-of-the-art security

system," Lucy started a spiel that sounded like she was a professional realtor. "Only the person meant to own the house can open the door."

She waited for Harriet to join her on the front porch.

"That's it? If she can open it, it's hers?" I asked. "And the other people just couldn't?"

"That's it," Lucy said. "It's pretty self-explanatory and makes my job a heck of a lot easier."

Harriet hesitated. "What if it opens, and I can't afford it?"

I hurried up beside her. "If it opens, and you want to live here, I'll do whatever I can to help you." Esme left me more money than any person needed, and Katie's husband, Earl, had helped me invest it. Basically, I was set, plus I was supposedly getting a large inheritance that technically should at least partially go to Harriet, too.

Lucy looked between the two of us. "Ready?"

Harriet bounced a bit on her toes, then started up the steps.

Lucy and I held our breath as she reached for the handle.

It turned easily in her hand, and the door swung open wide.

Harriet turned back to look at us with a huge smile. "Let's check it out."

15

Lucy's house had a sort of magic where it was much bigger on the inside than it looked from the outside. The house next door—the one Harriet was considering purchasing—was perhaps only slightly larger inside than it looked outside.

"I was worried it would be huge inside like yours," she said to Lucy. "That would be far too much space for me."

"This looks almost perfect for you," I said. "And it's so cozy. Does the furniture come with it?"

"The furniture is part of the staging, but if you want it to come with the house, it's an extra little bit," Lucy said.

"Depending on how much it is, I'd like to keep it in place," Harriet said. "The minimalistic look is exactly how I like it."

Every minimalistic house I'd been inside had seemed so cold with all the empty space. Here, you could feel the warmth radiating. Maybe it was the magic, or maybe it was just because the house was showing off for Harriet. I didn't know.

"I'd like to talk numbers," Harriet said to Lucy. "I didn't think it would happen so quickly, but I knew I wanted to settle down near Ellie."

She said it without a hint of emotion, but I had enough emotion streaming through my veins for the both of us.

"Oh, stop," Harriet said, glancing at my hair.

It turned a shimmery pink and twisted itself into long braids down both my shoulders. "You know I can't help it."

"You can control your emotions," Harriet said. "Maybe not your hair, but your emotions control your hair."

"If only it were that easy," I said. "Maybe I'd have a real family right now."

"Ouch," Harriet said.

"Not that—oh—I'm so sorry. I didn't mean it like that." I wrapped my arms around Harriet's neck before remembering she hated being hugged and dropping my arms back to my sides. "I meant that maybe one of the foster families would have kept me."

"It's their loss, dear," Lucy said. "Let's head back over to my place, and we can discuss the financials. I'll get the family on the phone and see what they'd be willing to do."

The house talk took the place of my magic lesson, but I didn't mind. I was just happy Harriet would stick around.

Even though I'd found a family in the Cliff Haven residents, it would still be nice to have a blood relative nearby. And Harriet had met my mother and grandmother.

She'd even met me right after I was born—before my mother left me at the fire station.

By the time the night was over, we'd settled a deal for the house that included the furniture and didn't require my financial assistance at all.

"I'm happy to help if you ever need it," I said to Harriet as we were driving away. "I know you probably don't like to ask for help—I'm the same way—but that's what family's for."

"Thank you for bringing me with you tonight," she said. "I didn't know it would end with me being a homeowner."

"It's almost like magic," I said, silently wondering if Lucy had planned it that way all along.

As we pulled into the driveway, Harriet didn't seem nearly as happy as I would have expected her to.

"What's the matter?"

"Why do you think something is the matter?" Harriet asked, but her smile faltered.

"Just a hunch."

"It's dumb, but I don't want to leave Wix," she said. "He's been such a good friend of mine since I arrived."

"Then take him with you," I said. "I'm sure Melly May would be perfectly okay with that."

"But then I'll only get more attached. He is not my dog."

She had a point there. "Then we'll get you a puppy."

"It won't be the same," she said. "Wix is a special animal."

If chewing up pillows and destroying everything when he wasn't walked made him special, he was special, all right. Otherwise, he was probably special to Harriet like Penelope was special to me.

"Let's sleep on it," I said. "It's been a big day. This isn't a decision we have to make tonight."

Harriet and I ambled up the steps, both tired from the day.

"Thank you, Ellie," Harriet said behind me.

I turned to find her with tears in her eyes. "It's my pleasure. Thank you for coming back."

She wrapped her arms around me and squeezed, then promptly let go and backed away. It was the best two-second hug I'd ever had.

Wix and Penelope greeted us at the door, both of their tails wagging.

Harriet sniffled beside me. I desperately wanted to wrap an arm around her and comfort her, but that would likely bring her more discomfort than anything, so I held off.

"Goodnight," I said, starting up the stairs with Penelope at my heels.

"Goodnight," Harriet said. "Thanks again."

16

"Today's the day, ladies," Coral was way too chipper so early in the morning.

Thankfully, she'd called me an hour and a half before I needed to be at the café for the early morning interviews. I wouldn't have been awake in time.

"Put on your game faces and get your speeches ready. The people want to hear from you. Tell them what they'll get if they elect you as Mayor for a Day."

Katie was right there with me, helping me through my bullet points. I was confident I could steer the reporters away from the magic perspective. She'd told me to explain my experience in foster homes growing up and to add humor with the story of me falling into the poop.

I wasn't sure about using the poop story, but both Katie and Coral thought it was gold. They said I had a knack for telling stories. That wasn't the first time someone had told me so, but it hadn't always been said positively.

The three of us wore more makeup than usual, sitting

at one long table facing five rows of empty chairs. Reporters crowded outside behind the locked door.

"Are you ready?" Coral asked.

We all nodded. I sat in the middle, which Katie said was the power seat. To me, it felt more like the hot seat. But maybe we all felt like that. Well, at least Laura and I. Andrea seemed only too prepared. I had to keep reminding myself she'd done this before and not too long ago. She knew what she was doing.

The reporters filed in quickly, taking their assigned seats.

Cameras began rolling after a countdown and the questions started.

A man in the front row, holding a pad of paper and a yellow number two pencil, said, "How are each of you feeling this morning?"

Andrea started. "It's good to see you again, Tom. Thank you for asking. I think we're all rather nervous but excited to start the festival off with the time-honored tradition of Mayor for a Day."

Dang. She was good.

Tom turned his eyes on me. "I'm feeling great," I said. "A bit tired, as it's still so early."

A couple of the reporters chuckled and nodded in agreement.

"I'm very excited about the festival. Most of all, for the shortcake decorating competition."

"That does sound like fun," Tom said without smiling. "And you?"

Laura hesitated. "I feel fine. I mean, great. I'm excited

too. I need decorations. I mean, the city needs decorations."

I felt bad that her nerves were getting the better of her.

"That's a great segue," the woman next to Tom said. "Why don't each of you tell us about your platforms? What change will you make when you're Mayor for a Day?"

Laura cleared her throat and recited a speech she'd probably only practiced in front of her mirror. "The town has been using the same decorations for years now. They're fine, but every year they become more worn. I try to fix them, but after a while, it becomes impossible. That's why, when I'm Mayor for a Day, I'll add brand new holiday and seasonal decorations to the town budget."

The woman looked pleased, and Laura looked relieved to get that off her chest.

"And you, Ellie?" the woman asked.

"If I'm elected Mayor for a Day, I'll add garbage cans and the staff to take care of those garbage cans into the town budget."

"That seems rather . . ." the woman searched for a word.

"Dull? Boring?" I laughed. "I know."

The other reporters laughed nervously.

"But you wouldn't think it was dull if you ended up covered in dog poop after trying to be the responsible foster pet parent by picking it up in one of those little poop baggies."

A couple of the women in the back gasped.

"That's what happened to me," I said, launching into the story that Coral and Katie said I told so well. Apparently, they were right because, by the time I'd finished, everyone was cracking up, and a couple of people in the front row were wiping tears from their eyes.

"If you're finished," Andrea said. "I'd like to talk about my rather more serious matter."

The room went silent. In the back, I saw Nick shake his head.

"When I'm elected Mayor for a Day, I will do away with the mayoral position in Cliff Haven."

The room erupted in questions and chatter. Could she do that? Was that even a possibility? What would become of Cliff Haven without a mayor?

All the same questions we'd had when she mentioned it, the reporters asked.

When my gaze met Nick's, he smiled and shrugged.

The questions were coming too quickly for Andrea to answer, and Coral ended up stepping in to stop the questions. She ended the press conference early with a schedule of events for the festival.

Once most of the reporters had filed out of the café, Katie hurried over to me.

"You did so well," she said. "You may be running a trash campaign, but you're doing it with grace and humor, and I couldn't be prouder. How about some crispy-edged pancakes?"

"I'd love some," I said. "And coffee too?"

"You act as if I don't know you at all." She hugged me quickly before heading to the back to put in my order. Katie owned the café, but Bex was the one who managed it. Currently, Bex was taking orders frantically from the people who had stayed for a bite to eat after the interviews.

I jumped in to help. It wasn't one of my scheduled workdays, but it would be silly to make Bex handle such a rush all by herself.

As I tied on my black half-apron with a notepad and a pen inside, Bex mouthed, "Thank you."

Within less than fifteen minutes, the entire place was packed and everyone's order was taken.

While we waited for the flood of orders to be ready for service from the kitchen, Bex and I stood toward the back near the circle table where all the local farmers from the community sat every morning.

"You did so well answering their questions. I would have been way nervous," Bex said. She wore bellbottom jeans with a cute blue peasant top and her black hair was in short twists.

"Katie helped get me ready," I said. "Plus, it's not like my campaign is life or death. If I don't win, I'll be okay."

"Will you, though?" Bex wiggled her eyebrows at me. She knew me too well.

"Okay, I want to win."

"That's my girl."

"Harriet's back," I said as I refilled Earl and Hank's coffee mugs.

"Really?" Bex's voice was filled with distrust.

"She's buying a house," I said.

"In town?"

"Just outside of town." Cliff Hallow was a magical town, and Bex wasn't a witch, so I hadn't told her about it.

"That'll be nice to have her close," she said. "Did she ever figure out who was trying to kill her?"

"She thinks it's a moot point." I shrugged. "I'm just really glad she's here."

Bex searched me for any clue hinting at how I was really feeling. "I guess I am too."

The bell on the door chimed, and Bex and I both looked to find Xander standing there. The last time I saw him, I'd made a massive fool of myself—almost falling into his arms. "I—uh—think some of the food might be up." I hurried off to the kitchen as my scalp tingled.

I tied my hair up into a bun and secured it with a large, colorful scrunchie in hopes people wouldn't notice it changing color—that Xander wouldn't notice it changing color.

"What was that all about?" Bex asked, coming up behind me and making me jump.

"Nothing," I said. "I'm just trying to stay out of Laura's way."

She put her hands on her hips.

"Fine," I said. "I made a gigantic fool of myself a couple of days ago. I thought Xander was holding his arms open to comfort me, but he was there to comfort Laura. Of course, because she's his girlfriend, right? But I may have made it obvious that I was about to walk into his embrace, and then I may have let my emotions get the best of me and teleported home."

Bex's eyes widened, and her jaw hung open.

"I know," I said. "It was hugely embarrassing."

"I'm not shocked because of your reaction to Xander,"

she said. "I'm shocked because you never told me you can teleport."

"I didn't know," I said. "And Lucy and Renée were just as surprised as me." I left out the part about Esme's journal and how Esme had teleported too.

"So that's not a normal witchy thing to do?" Bex asked.

"Apparently not," I said.

"I am so glad I'm not a witch. It would freak me out if one moment I was here and the next I was somewhere else."

"Uh, yeah, it's pretty freaky."

"Sorry, El. That was insensitive."

Before I could reply, one of the Charlies—two worked at the café as chefs—rang the bell, notifying us that the food was ready to be delivered.

"Charlie, we're standing right here," Bex shouted.

"Sorry, habit," Charlie said and went back to flipping pancakes. "These are for you, Ellie. Hurry and deliver your food so you can eat."

"I can take it from here," Bex said. "Thank you for the help. I'll give you the tips from your tables."

"Keep 'em," I said. "I only took the orders."

Charlie handed me a plate of the most gorgeous-looking, crispy-edged pancakes with a large scoop of butter right in the center.

I took my plate to the dining area, but there was no place to sit.

"You can sit with us," Earl said, patting a chair next to him.

Just as I sat, Katie appeared with a cup of coffee and

syrup. "Thanks for helping Bex. I was on the phone. I'll get some orders delivered."

I smiled up at her.

"I hear you're looking for some trash cans in the square," Earl said. Earl was a surly older man on the outside with a gooey center. It was finding the center that was difficult sometimes. He was also Katie's husband.

"Yep," I said. "I'm tired of carrying around a bag of poop."

"Especially when you end up covered in it, right?" Hank said with a laugh. Hank looked like a rock-n-roll Santa Claus with white hair, beard, and jolly red cheeks. The rock-n-roll part came from the tattoos and leather he occasionally wore.

"Especially then," I said. "But let's not talk about that while I'm eating."

They laughed and talked about their fields and what stage of planting they were in. I owned a large field that Hank rented and farmed. He was the most polite farmer ever—making sure I was okay with him coming over, paying me on time, and never making a mess of the driveway or yard.

I took a gooey bite of pancakes mixed with butter and syrup and closed my eyes. The crispy edges gave it the perfect texture. I savored it. When I opened my eyes, Xander was standing right next to me.

"Good pancakes?" he asked.

"The best," I said, not looking up at him.

"We need to talk."

"About what?"

"We can't talk about it here."

"I'm eating." I glanced over to where Laura was giving me the evil eye. "And your girlfriend looks uncomfortable with you being over here."

"She knows we're friends."

I glanced up at him. He had a worried expression on his face.

"Fine, let's talk. After I'm done eating."

"I'll meet you at your house this afternoon."

My stomach felt like it was full of butterflies. Suddenly, I wasn't so hungry after all. "Sounds like a plan."

17

I'd never been so nervous to see a man in my life. What did he want to talk about? Had he proposed to Laura? Was he going to propose to Laura?

I checked my reflection for the millionth time to make sure I looked semi-presentable and waited in the window seat for him to arrive.

Penelope oinked a little. I reached down and picked her up. I must have been daydreaming because I heard the doorbell ring before I saw Xander.

I checked my reflection once more before opening the door.

"Hey," Xander said.

How did he look so good? Would there ever be a time I wasn't insanely attracted to him, or was he just so gorgeous I'd always notice?

"Come on in," I said. Penelope nuzzled against his legs, and he reached down to pet her as he stepped inside.

"Are you sure Laura's okay with you being over here?"

"She understands our situation," he said. "Plus, this

goes beyond her feelings. Why didn't you tell me you teleported?"

Oh, that. Better than him announcing his engagement.

"I talked to Lucy and Renée about it," I said. "I didn't think I needed a third opinion."

"But I'm . . ." He hesitated. "Your friend."

"Things have just been different lately, which is okay," I added quickly. "But since the caves and then Laura and Bernardo, it's just . . . weird."

He shoved his hands in the pockets of his jeans and rocked back on his heels. "I know, but that doesn't mean I'm not here for you."

I shrugged. "I figured if Lucy and Renée hadn't ever heard of a witch teleporting, you probably wouldn't have either."

"Actually, I have," he said.

"You have? Like in recent history?"

"Very," he said. "Your grandmother could teleport."

"She told you that?"

"You don't seem surprised."

"I may have found that out on my own."

"Did Harriet tell you?"

I shook my head. "Harriet and I haven't had much time to talk with her buying the house and everything."

"Wait, Harriet's buying a house?"

"In Cliff Hallow next to Lucy's," I said. "She thinks I'm no longer in danger from Monroe because if I'm the next Grand Witch, I'll immediately get the inheritance."

"She told you all that?" Xander didn't look surprised by any of this.

"Did you already know?" I asked.

"About what?"

"About Monroe no longer being after Harriet? Or me?" I shrugged, frustration edging into my scalp. "About me getting the entire inheritance if I become Grand Witch?"

"Yes."

"Why didn't you tell me?"

"I couldn't," he said. "If I'd have told you about the inheritance, it might have changed your mind about becoming Grand Witch."

"Like a bribe or something?" I asked. "I thought you knew me better than that. Money means nothing to me. And I already have so much of it, I don't need more."

"It's still against the rules."

I sighed. "So about the teleporting . . ."

"Did you mean to do it?"

"No," I said. "I just wished I was home."

"You wished you were home. Then, poof, you were home?"

Penelope oinked up at us.

"Basically."

"If you wanted to, could you do it again right now?"

"Probably not."

"Why not?"

"Because I'm not upset."

"You were upset?"

Seriously, guys could be so dense. Or maybe he was simply trying to spare my feelings.

"Is that why you ran out of the room? It was because of the deaths, right?"

"Uh, yeah," I said. "I was just overwhelmed with it all."

"Laura was pretty shaken up about it too," he said. "So, you got upset, wished you were home, then you were?"

"Pretty much."

"Interesting."

"Could my grandmother control her teleportation?" I asked.

"Eventually, yes," he said. "But it took her a while to hone the skill, just like it takes a while to hone any magical skill."

"You're telling me. I still haven't figured out how to use my magic to clean the house." I laughed.

"I'm sorry you felt like you couldn't confide in me," Xander said. "I don't want to lose our friendship just because we had a moment, and now we're seeing other people."

A moment? Is that what he called practically making out and him telling me he wanted to be with me before running back to Laura? I pushed the thoughts away when Penelope oinked again, notifying me that my hair was changing.

"It's really okay," I said. "I know you're busy with—well—whatever you're busy with. And Renée is the current Grand Witch, so it only makes sense I'd go to her if she has the time."

"Yes," he said slowly. "But I still want to know what's happening in your life."

My frustration level was rising. He wanted to be friends. He wanted to know about my life. It was all about take, take, take with him. He never told me anything about his life.

"It's all good," I said. "Lucy and Renée—and now Harriet—have it covered."

Xander tried to object, but I cut him off.

"I have a client before my next scheduled event for the Strawberry Festival," I said. "But thanks for coming over."

He looked torn.

I opened the door and waited for him to exit.

He might have wanted to say more, but he didn't. Which was probably for the best.

I needed to focus on getting over him. Maybe when the festival was over, I'd take a little trip down to Argentina.

18

I headed out to the barn to get ready for my session with a new client complaining of shoulder tension. Bex had helped me set up an online scheduling form where I could block out the times I wasn't available, and people could sign up on my website instead of trying to get in touch with me on the phone.

I wasn't a terribly reliable cell phone carrier. I'd never really had a reason to have a phone on me at all times until I came to Cliff Haven and made friends.

Either way, the online scheduler was nice because people could put in as much or as little information as possible, pay for the session upfront, and I'd get a handy little notification in my inbox, text messages, and on my calendar. I just had to make sure I checked my schedule regularly.

The barn had been transformed into the exercise studio of my dreams. One day, practically the entire town showed up to help me clean it up and make it into what it was now.

I sectioned the front and the back off with a heavy curtain spanning the barn crossways to hide the mural, which was still of the diner. Though, now, it was daytime again.

I reached up and touched the paint, but there were no magical specks today.

"Ellie?" A woman's voice came from the doorway. "Am I in the right place?"

I came out from behind the curtain with a big smile on my face. "Welcome to Relief with Ellie—oh—hi, Andrea."

"Hey," she said, hesitating in the doorway. "Is this too weird with us being competitors? If it is, I can go. I just have this terrible tension in my shoulder, and you're the only one in town who—"

"It's not weird at all," I said. "I'm glad you came in."

"You won't try to sabotage me or anything, right?" She let out a nervous laugh. This might have been the first time I'd ever seen her in anything but a pantsuit. And she had a smile on her face.

"That probably wouldn't be very good for my business if I went around doing more damage than good—even to a competitor."

"True." She took another step inside, letting the door close behind her.

"You said you have some neck tension."

"It's nearly unbearable. Between that and Susan's death, I can hardly sleep. My movement is so limited I'm worried it'll start affecting the rest of my body."

"Let's assess your range of motion first so we can track the progress we make."

I talked her through some tests as I took notes on her movement.

"Do you mind if I touch you?" I asked as she started her stretches. "Just on your shoulders to deepen the stretch?"

She darted away from me. "Yes. Sorry, I do."

"No problem," I said, lifting my hands in the air. "It's not a requirement. It simply helps deepen the stretch."

Obviously, I couldn't come out and tell her my touch had magical healing properties and could ease the tension without as much stretching.

She hesitated before going back into the stretch as if I might pounce on her. Was she really someone who didn't like to be touched? Or was it because she was trying to hide her magic from me?

The magic was less noticeable on her today, but I could still sense it.

"Do you really want to get rid of the mayoral position completely?" I asked, trying to take her mind off the tension in her neck as she moved into another stretch.

"The mayor is all for show, and Nick is the biggest showboat I've ever seen. If we're not careful, he'll run the town into the ground."

"If it's all for show, how could he run it into the ground?" I asked, keeping my tone light.

"Okay, maybe it's not all for show," she admitted. "He has control of a large part of the town budget, and the first thing he did when he got into office was put up that stupid statue."

I still didn't know what statue she was referring to. "What's the matter with this statue? I haven't seen it."

"You should be thankful for that," Andrea said, moving her head back and forth with a greater range of motion than she had at the beginning. "A woman from Poppy Hills created the statue."

"Poppy Hills? That doesn't seem like something Nick would do. He seems like a Cliffer through and through."

"He is," Andrea said. "Susan thought he was sleeping with her."

"Had you and Susan been friends a long time?"

Andrea's eyes glazed over with tears. "She was my campaign manager when I ran against Nick. We became good friends."

I almost laughed at the idea of Nick's ex-wife being another person's campaign manager in a race against him.

"Do you know if she was really having an affair with Deacon?"

Andrea didn't reply right away. "Is this official or off the record?"

"I won't tell anyone unless it has something to do with the case."

"I'd say it has everything to do with the case," Andrea said. "Laura nailed it right on the head."

"You think Nick killed them because they were sleeping together? Even after he and Susan were divorced?"

"Nick never got over Susan." Andrea winced.

"If the stretch becomes painful, back out of it. We don't want to injure you more."

She did as I said, then continued, "That's why Susan thought he hired that woman to do the sculpture, to get back at her for sleeping with Deacon."

"Sounds complicated," I said.

"It was—is—I don't know. I don't envy the police for the position they're in trying to figure this case out."

We worked on some more stretches with minimal discussion.

"I think that concludes our session," I said as we finished the stretches. "How does your neck feel?"

Andrea moved with far more range of motion than she had at the beginning of the session.

"It feels better," she said. "Will it stay this way?"

I handed her a few printouts. "If you do these exercises one or two times a day, especially when you're stressed, it'll help keep you limber."

She reached for her jacket and, as she put it on, her car keys fell to the ground. I reached down to pick them up for her, but she was already reaching.

When our fingers touched, a jolt of electricity went through me.

She picked up the keys and smiled. I did my best to smile back. The keys in her hand sparkled in the light with traces of green glitter.

"Thanks for your help," she said. "I'll see you this afternoon in the square, right?"

I nodded.

When she was out of the barn, I sucked in a deep breath. I knew from our touch that Andrea had been lying about something. The green glitter confirmed it for me.

I needed to call Jake.

19

The square was festively decorated with all things strawberry. Laura had agreed to help Coral with the planning and decorating, though Coral seemed to go along with most of Laura's ideas.

"Over there, we'll have the carnival rides," Laura pointed to the northwest street corner. "They'll go on the street with the Ferris wheel front and center. The Cliff Haven Strawberry Festival sign will hang in the center."

Coral nodded and made notes on her clipboard.

"What about the strawberry shortcake tower?" Coral asked.

"Center of the square." Laura glanced at her watch. "I think we need to get to the podiums."

Coral's face was red, and her hair was out of place. "I don't know how I would have managed this without you. Small towns are not really in my wheelhouse. I'm more suited for the big city."

"Maybe your family shouldn't have purchased the Cliff

Haven Strawberry Farm if this wasn't in your wheel-house," a male voice said behind me.

I turned to find Nick.

"I didn't realize when they purchased the farm that I would end up being their personal event planner." Coral looked at the buzzing phone in her hand. "Gah, speaking of. My sister is probably calling to put off the headshots again." She answered the phone. "Do not tell me you're cancelling on me again."

She walked away and Nick turned his attention to me. "How are you today, Ellie?"

"I'm okay," I said slowly. Why was he being nice to me?

"Great," he said. "Are you ready for the debates?"

My throat went dry. "Debates?" I squeaked out.

"Didn't you read the schedule?" Laura asked. "It's all there. We're debating our issues today."

"But I thought we already debated our issues at the diner."

"Those were interviews," Coral said, rejoining the group. "These debates will be much more heated. The crowd will love it."

"Crowd?" With each passing word, I got more and more worried.

"Practically the entire town will be here," Nick said. "Just like when they came to the debate between Andrea and me."

I hadn't been to that debate. In fact, I hadn't even known it was a thing. Right then and there, I made it my mission to get more familiar with the town's politics. If I was going to live here, I needed to make it my business.

"Speaking of Andrea," Coral said. "Has anyone seen her?"

I couldn't tell them she'd been at my house that day for a session—confidentiality and all.

Laura shrugged but didn't look directly at anyone.

"No one's seen her then?" Nick asked, his voice giddy as he checked his watch. "That means she's no longer one of the Mayor for a Day candidates."

"I guess you don't have to worry about losing your mayoral position," Coral said, though she didn't sound pleased about it.

Nick practically skipped along as he led the way to the stage in the middle of the square. Three podiums stood with each of our campaign signs we'd made the first day in class. The green glitter was not only on Laura's sign—a sign that featured me prominently in a trash can covered in garbage with a pointy black hat atop my head—Andrea's sign also had some green glitter along the borders.

That could mean that either of them might be responsible for Deacon and Susan's deaths.

"What's up with your sign?" Laura asked. "These were supposed to be slander signs. And you practically slandered yourself."

"I couldn't, in good faith, slander anyone else," I said.

Andrea's sign slandered each of the four other candidates equally. Maybe that meant she hadn't hurt Deacon and Susan. Though, if she'd left them off her sign, it might have instantly cast suspicion on her.

Nick was only too happy to take Andrea's sign off the front of her podium and rip it in half.

Laura took her place behind her podium. "I suppose we should get prepared for the debate."

My palms went instantly sweaty. I'd done well yesterday, but I had a feeling I wouldn't do as well today. I was not good at confrontation and hadn't prepared to argue for my side over hers.

"Don't worry about it," Nick said. "Running a clean campaign is always the way to go. You did the right thing."

The crowd was already forming. "I don't know how to debate," I said to Nick. "I never took that class in high school, and it wasn't exactly a high priority when I took my GED."

"You didn't finish high school?" Nick asked.

I shook my head. "It didn't keep me from going to college. I was a foster kid. When I turned sixteen, I decided enough was enough. I didn't want to go to another foster home, so I bought Mona and exited the system."

"Color me impressed, Vanderwick." Nick smiled.

"Why are you being nice to me?" I asked.

"I'm not." His smile instantly faded. "Just trying to be cordial. Especially if you end up winning this thing. You and I will have to work together a bit to get those trash cans." He looked down at the sign in his hands. "Which— I have to admit—would come in quite handy right now."

I didn't trust his kindness for one second, but I didn't have time to question it. He walked away, leaving me to figure out what the heck I would say in the debate.

"I regret to inform you," Nick said into the microphone, the enormous crowd listening intently, "that Andrea is no longer a candidate for Mayor for a Day. The debate will be between Laura and Ellie. Either way, your vote will change the look of the town—one with shiny new festive decorations and the other with ugly trash cans that will take care of the non-existent dog poop."

"Hey," I said, irritation rising in my voice.

Nick winked at me, then walked off the stage.

At least he was back to being his usual mean self.

Laura and I stood behind each of our podiums. They'd been pushed closer together after Andrea's had been removed. She still hadn't shown up. Probably because Jake had taken her into jail after I told him about the green glitter. I'd feel terrible if my accusation ruined her chance to become Mayor for a Day.

Coral took her place, seated at a desk off to the side of the stage. "Welcome, everyone. I'm Coral Bell. I'll be your moderator for today's debate."

The crowd cheered, and Coral blushed.

"We'll start with introductions," she said. "Will each of you introduce yourselves and your campaign platforms, starting with Laura?"

Laura smirked at me, then looked out at the crowd with more confidence than I'd ever seen in her. As she spoke, her face warmed, and her smile became more natural. It was then I realized she was looking at Xander. And he was returning her adoring stare.

My heart felt like it dropped from my chest into my stomach at the sight of him. Frustration crept up my spine. Tingles began on the edge of my hairline.

No.

I would not let my hair change.

Not now.

It would look like I was trying to take the focus off Laura. And though that was exactly what I wanted to do, it would be petty.

I sucked in a deep breath. When I glanced back up, Xander's eyes were no longer trained on his girlfriend but on me. More specifically—my hair.

No one else in the crowd seemed to notice anything.

If only I had a mirror so I could see what he was looking at.

When his gaze shifted down to meet mine, I gave him a questioning expression, but he glanced away.

"And you, Ellie?" Coral asked from her desk.

Shoot, it was my turn, and I wasn't ready.

I sucked in a deep breath and let the words tumble from my mouth.

"I'm not proposing anything as crazy as getting rid of the mayoral position. Or anything as glamorous as new decorations. All I want is trash cans. So, when someone's dog needs to go to the bathroom, it's easier to pick up the waste and throw it away."

I glanced at Laura. "But I understand if you'd rather have nicer decorations for the town. I wish we could both get what we want because I know they'd both do a lot of good for the town. Thank you."

Cheers erupted from the crowd.

Laura gaped at me.

Xander clapped, ignoring Laura's glares.

"What a wonderful opening statement," Coral said. "Now, shall we get into the debate questions?"

20

The debate was a total dud. I'd extinguished any chance of it being exciting when I'd basically said I wanted us both to win.

"What was that?" Laura asked, pulling me behind the stage after we'd said our last statements. "I drew you in a trash can and a witch's hat, and you tell everyone you want us both to win?"

"I don't know," I said, exasperated. "I guess it occurred to me that both of our ideas were good ones."

"But that's not how this works," Laura said. "One of us is supposed to win, and one is supposed to lose. You can't go off saying we should both win."

"Just because I said we should both win doesn't mean we will," I said. "Everyone will vote, and only one of us will win."

"You," she practically screamed. "You will win because *you* seem like the nice one. The sweet one. Everyone loves *you*. Do you know how long I practiced for this debate? For this candidacy? And you come in at the eleventh hour spewing garbage about trash cans. I thought for sure the other three would be my biggest competition. I never thought our town was stupid enough to fall for your doe-eyed expression and pacifist personality."

"Is everything okay over here?" Xander asked, coming to stand by Laura's side.

"Everything is fine," Laura said. "Let's go."

They walked away hand-in-hand, but I wasn't jealous. Not this time. This time, I was suspicious.

"Hey, Ellie," Jake said. "That was great up there."

"Thanks," I said. "I'm really glad you came over. Did you get any information out of Andrea?"

Jake shook his head slowly. "I didn't find her. I thought maybe she'd show up here."

"She couldn't have gone far," I said. "Did you check her house?"

"That was my first stop," Jake said.

"Anything else on the case?"

He shook his head. "Nothing new."

"I think Laura might need to be looked at more closely."

Jake laughed, then realized I wasn't smiling. "Laura? As in *that* Laura?" He pointed to where she and Xander were laughing about something together, their heads close and their fingers intertwined.

"That's the only Laura I know," I said. "And yes, that one."

"The one who's dating the guy you're secretly in love with?"

"I'm not secretly in love with Xander."

"So, you told him?"

"I'm dating his cousin."

"His cousin in a different country?" Jake laughed and shook his head.

"This has nothing to do with Xander," I said. "Laura just came over and told me she thought the other three were her biggest competition—you know, the three who are dead and missing?"

"I'll talk to her," Jake said. "But first, we need to find Andrea."

Jake and I searched the square, but the crowd had mostly cleared out, leaving it pretty easy to determine that Andrea wasn't there.

Just as we were about to head to back to her house, I got a text from an unknown number on my phone.

Leave Jake and meet me by the Ferris wheel

I glanced around, trying to figure out who'd sent me such a cryptic message, but found no one. I texted back.

Who is this?

The response came almost immediately.

Neve

I texted my response.

Be right there.

"Hey, Jake," I said. "I think I'll take a rain check on heading to Andrea's house. Let me know if you find her, okay?"

Jake looked at me, his piercing blue eyes boring holes into my skull. "Okay," he said slowly. "And you let me know if you figure out anything."

"I don't think I will," I said. "Too busy with all this campaigning."

He nodded like he didn't believe me. He may not have been magical, but he could see right through me sometimes. "Stay away from Laura. I'm pretty sure she didn't do this."

"She put me on her sign, but not Andrea," I said as he walked toward his truck. "Maybe because she knew Andrea wouldn't be here."

"Or maybe she just hates you," Jake said with a laugh.

When I didn't reply, he threw up a hand in goodbye. I watched as he got into his truck and drove away before walking as casually as I could to the Ferris wheel. It had just been delivered to the corner where Laura had planned.

As I approached, I could see Neve's magical trace. She was on the other side.

"Hey," I said, coming around.

She jumped.

"Sorry, I didn't mean to scare you."

"It's okay," she said, smoothing down the wrinkles in her pants. "There's something I need to tell you, but you can't say anything to anyone."

"If I can't say anything to anyone, how can I help in this situation?"

"I just need you to know. And maybe you'll be able to get more information or clues or something."

Neve was not only a regular coroner; she was a magical coroner. Though she wasn't certified to be one. But even without the certification, she could still determine when someone was killed magically.

"You know how it seemed like Susan died of suicide?"

"Yes," I said.

"And how Deacon was shot?"

"With the gun next to Susan."

"But Susan died before she was tied up to the stall."

"Right," I said. "Jake told me."

"Which would mean she probably didn't kill Deacon."

I nodded. This was all well within the realm of possibility.

"The thing is, they were both killed by someone magical." She exhaled as if telling me took a literal load off her shoulders.

"But Deacon was shot with the gun next to Susan?"

"The bullets had magical traces on them."

I started to pull out my phone, but Neve stopped me.

"What are you doing?"

"Calling Jake."

"You can't tell him."

"I won't tell him what you told me, but I need him to know what he might walk into."

"What do you mean?"

"He's trying to find Andrea," I said, then lowered my

voice to a whisper. "And Andrea is magical, but she doesn't want anyone to know."

Neve gasped. "But you could tell?"

"I don't know how or why, but apparently, I have a thing about seeing magic on people who don't want others to know they're magical."

"And she's the only one you saw who was magical?"

"Other than you?" I whispered.

She slapped a hand over my mouth.

"Sorry," I said, my voice muffled by her hand.

She let me go. "Anyone else?"

"No, why?"

"Deacon was a warlock," she said. "But his disguise was nearly flawless. I didn't realize it until I reached his heart."

"His heart?"

"Witch and warlock hearts differ slightly from human hearts. I won't go into the details—and a non-magical coroner wouldn't notice—but to me, it's plain as day."

"Deacon was magical, which probably means his mother is too," I said.

"His mother is here?" Neve glanced around, her eyes wide.

"His mother is the one who nominated him."

"Are you certain?" Neve asked. "Maybe it was a family friend? Or a stepmother?"

"She called herself his mom. That's all I know. Why?"

She looked around to make sure we were still alone. "Deacon's mother was murdered years ago. And Deacon was the prime suspect, but they couldn't get enough evidence to convict him."

"Wow," I said. "Was this a secret among the magical community?"

"No, why?"

"Xander said nothing about Deacon being a suspected murderer," I said. "I'm just surprised he let Laura anywhere near someone like that."

"Maybe it was because Deacon was going by a different name. His real name is Monroe."

"Monroe?" My stomach dropped. I'd only heard that name once before.

"But Xander should have known—wait—why do you look like that?"

"Look like what?" I asked.

"Like you're going to pass out."

"Because Deacon—Monroe—was my cousin."

21

Neve looked at me with massive brown eyes. "What do you mean, he was your cousin?"

"I never met him, but Harriet—my other cousin—told me about him. He killed his mom and her mom and possibly even my mom and then tried to come after us, too."

"And now he's dead," Neve said.

"Just like that?" I was talking to myself more than Neve. "It seems too easy."

"Someone magical killed him," Neve said. "Do you think your cousin—do you think Harriet—"

"No." I stopped her from finishing her sentence but knew her train of thought paralleled mine. "I can't think that. She couldn't have."

"I don't think I've met Harriet. Is she new to town?"

"She just bought a place in Cliff Hallow. She said everything was okay, and we didn't need to worry about Monroe anymore."

The silence between us was heavy. If Harriet had killed

Monroe, she definitely wouldn't have walked into my life so casually, would she?

"I think you should talk to Jake about it," Neve said.

"How do I do that when I'm not supposed to know Deacon was magical? Or my cousin?"

"Talk to his mom—or the woman claiming to be his mom—maybe she'll slip up and give you the information."

That was a good idea. "I still need to tell Jake to watch out for Andrea," I said. "She's a witch. She could have killed them, too."

"It's possible," Neve said. "But I thought Andrea and Susan were friends."

"Maybe she had a thing for Deacon and killed them both?"

We considered this for a moment.

"Why use magic on the bullets?" I asked. "It wasn't like Deacon—Monroe—was immortal. And that just left a trace, so you would know they used magic."

"Honestly, if I couldn't do the things I can do—ahem—in my professional capacity, a regular coroner wouldn't have been able to tell the difference in the bodies or the bullets. But when I figured out Deacon was magical, I took a little trip to the crime scene investigation lab. It only took a quick glance to see the magic on the bullets."

"How can you see magic on objects?"

She shrugged. "They taught it in my training."

I frowned at her. "Magical coroner training? If you're trained to be a coroner in the magical community, why aren't you working as one?"

She turned from me. "I have to get back to work." And with that, she was gone.

Since I didn't know where Deacon's mom—or whoever she was—lived, I decided to visit my living cousin. Mona got me to Harriet's door in a matter of minutes, using her magical speed. The house looked completely different from when we'd first looked at it.

It was more . . . Harriet.

The lawn was meticulously cut and the perfect shade of green, which looked slightly hilarious against Lucy's bright pink grass. Every bit of character the previous owners had put into the exterior of Harriet's house—the cute little garden gnomes, the welcome sign on the door, even the blue shutters—were gone.

Harriet's home had its own character in its normalcy. It stood out against the more outlandish magical homes surrounding it. I knocked on the freshly painted white door with the gold door knocker.

Harriet opened the door, beaming.

My heart sank. How could I come into her new home —her sanctuary—and accuse her of murdering our cousin?

The thought caught me off guard. Is that what I was here to do? That's not what I had intended to do. At least not consciously.

"Did you forget why you came?" Harriet asked.

My train of thought derailed, flew over the side of a cliff, and exploded. "Uh, no. I just wanted to see your new house."

"You could have called first."

That was hilarious, coming from the one person who never called before visiting me.

Harriet stepped out of the way to let me in. "Are you going to come in or just stand outside?"

"Thanks," I said, suddenly unsure of myself in her presence. I desperately wanted her to be innocent of the crime, but she'd told me she was going to kill him the last time she was in town. She said it was either him or her.

"Do you like it?" Harriet asked.

"What?" I asked.

"My house."

I glanced around at the minimalistic and neutral decor. "It's nice. Do you like it?"

Harriet smiled again. "I do. It's exactly what I've imagined. My mother decorated far too frivolously. A home should be a retreat from excess, a place to exhale. I finally feel like I can relax."

"I'm glad," I said.

"You didn't come to see the house, did you?" Harriet asked.

It would be better to just get it out in the open. "I came because Monroe is dead."

"I know." Harriet didn't blink—didn't make any expression other than drop her smile.

"Why didn't you tell me?"

"I did tell you." She looked confused. "Plus, you're the one who found him."

"I didn't know Deacon was Monroe. And you never told me he was dead."

"I told you he wouldn't be a problem anymore."

"Because I was going to inherit the money if I become Grand Witch."

She didn't meet my eye. She'd misled me on purpose.

"Did you kill him?" I asked before I could stop myself.

"No," she said. "But I wish I had."

Even though I wasn't touching her, I knew she was telling the truth. "Do you know who did?"

"No, but whoever did must have been a very powerful witch or warlock. Monroe has escaped death many times over."

Or maybe they caught him off-guard.

"Do you know anything about his mother?" I asked.

"The woman who birthed him or the woman who claims to be his mother now?" Harriet sat on one of her beige couches, and I followed suit.

"Either? Both?"

"He killed his birth mother the moment he knew he'd have to compete with her to get our grandfather's money," she said. "Right around the same time he killed my mother, and yours went missing."

"And the other woman?"

"She was his nanny growing up," Harriet said. "She practically raised him, so it's no surprise he thinks of her as his mother."

"Is she a witch?"

"Yes," Harriet said. "But not one powerful enough to kill him."

"Susan wasn't a witch," I said. "The woman he was with."

"Are you certain?" Harriet asked.

I hadn't asked Neve, but I figured she would have brought it up if Susan was a witch. "Pretty certain."

"Maybe she's a charm-chaser."

"A what?" I laughed.

"A charm-chaser," she said again, not finding the humor in the name. "A non-magical person who only dates someone with magic."

I laughed again. "She was married to a non-magical guy."

"Was," Harriet said. "Maybe she decided the magic life was more her speed."

Charm-chaser—maybe that's what Laura was.

"But Monroe certainly wasn't only dating one woman," she said. "He left a string of tears in the wake of his death. I suspect his funeral will be packed with all the women he left behind."

"When is the funeral?" I asked.

"Doesn't matter," Harriet said. "We won't be invited."

"If someone killed Deacon and Susan, maybe they did it out of jealousy."

"And you think that someone will be at his funeral?"

"It's worth a shot," I said. "Do you know when it is and how we can get in?"

"I know the details, yes," she said. "You're the future Grand Witch of the States. If you really want to go, that's our admission ticket."

22

The funeral was taking place the next day. I had to rearrange a couple of Mayor for a Day things with Katie. Apparently, the headshots had been postponed anyway. The election was less than twenty-four hours away—right at the opening of the Strawberry Festival—and Katie was sure I'd already punched my ticket with or without headshots.

Harriet gave Mona the directions, and I let her take over the driving as she bolted away from Cliff Haven to the west toward Des Moines.

"I'm not convinced Monroe's killer will be at his funeral. If they were mad enough to kill him and Susan, wouldn't they be mad enough not to attend his funeral?"

I shrugged. "I've seen it on TV. The killer is always at the funeral."

"Those TV shows are as fake as they come. We're wasting our time doing this."

I glanced over at her. "Is there another reason you don't want to go to his funeral?"

She looked out the window in silence long enough for the space between us to become awkward.

Just as I was about to apologize for butting into her personal life, she whispered, "They're all going to think I did it."

"Are you afraid for your life?"

She didn't look at me. "They won't hurt me as long as I'm with you."

Anger rose in me. "Who are they? How about I talk to them so they won't hurt you whether you're with me or not?"

Harriet whipped around to look at me. "Are you getting angry?"

If the tingles in my scalp were any indication, my hair could answer that question without me uttering a peep. "You're my only living relative. My only real family. No one is going to hurt you."

"I'm not worried," she said. "And I shouldn't worry what they think of me, either. If given the opportunity, I would have killed him."

I sighed. "Please stop saying that. And do not tell the police that if they question you."

"The police are off looking for someone non-magical," Harriet said.

"Jake knows there's the possibility it could be someone magical," I said. I'd given him a heads-up when I called him the day before. He hadn't found Andrea at her house.

"Why would you do that?" she asked, though her voice wasn't angry or worried, just its usual monotone. "Wait, how did you figure out that Deacon was Monroe?"

Panic rose in my chest. I was a terrible liar. "That's confidential."

Harriet narrowed her eyes at me. "Are you working with a magical coroner?"

I didn't answer. I couldn't lie, but I also couldn't tell her the truth.

"You are, aren't you?"

I stared ahead at the scenery passing us by at super-speed, almost as if the world was fast-forwarding.

"Which one?"

"How many are there?" I asked, trying to deflect her questioning with my own questions.

"Not many," Harriet said. "I could narrow it down if you don't want to tell me."

"I don't want to tell you," I said. "I can't tell you."

She sat back in her seat with a look of determination in her eyes. "I will figure it out."

"Why does it matter so much?"

"Magical coroners are almost as rare as Grand Witch-es," she said. "If you know one, it's like knowing a celebrity."

"I didn't take you as someone who cares much about knowing celebrities."

"Not real celebrities, no."

I stopped asking. Neve didn't want to talk about why she was no longer a magical coroner. Maybe she'd never actually been a certified one. Or maybe something had happened.

"Looks like we're here," I said as Mona slowed to a stop behind a line of vehicles that stretched as far as I could see, leading to a massive structure.

"Mona, can you drop us off and park yourself?" Harriet asked.

I gaped at her. "I don't think she—"

Mona's steering wheel warmed in my hands, and her engine revved a bit. "Okay, maybe she can."

"If you tell her to, she can," Harriet said. "Just use your magic."

My magic wasn't powering Mona.

She was her own being. And I loved her for it.

"How's Wix?" Harriet asked as we inched closer to the building.

"He's good," I said. "Hasn't ripped up a pillow in days."

"Still carting around his poop in little bags?"

"For now," I said. "But when I win, there will finally be trash cans in the square."

"Just in time for Melly May to get out of jail and Wix to go home with her."

I shrugged. "They'll be good for the town nonetheless."

"Do you think I could come by and visit sometime?" I'd never heard Harriet's voice so unsure—vulnerable.

"Of course," I said. "You're always welcome to visit. I thought you knew that by now."

"I learned something yesterday," Harriet said.

"Care to tell me what?" I asked when she didn't finish the statement.

"I learned the value of having someone call before coming over." She raised her eyebrows at me.

I laughed. "Point taken. I'll call next time."

"And I will too."

When Mona reached the front of the building, she slowed to a stop and opened our doors for us.

"Now, you're just showing off," Harriet said to me.

I smiled and squeezed Mona's wheel. "Someone is."

A mixture of black and color flowed into the auditorium. When I'd arrived at Harriet's wearing a black dress, she practically yelled at me. Apparently, at magical funerals, wearing black means you're non-magical. And the possible future Grand Witch could not go to a magical funeral looking like she was non-magical.

Mona took us home, and I changed into a dress with purple swirls and a few sequins here and there. It wasn't the most colorful thing I had in my closet, but it seemed irreverent to go to a funeral wearing something bright.

When Harriet shrugged off her jacket, she wore a pale-yellow pantsuit. She definitely fit in more than I did.

Most of the seats in the room were already taken, but we found a couple just off the aisle.

"We'll want to make a quick exit when it's over," Harriet said.

"We can't," I said. "I have to be here to observe."

Harriet shifted in her seat.

I rested a hand on hers. I was trying to reassure her, but emotion flowed through me so quickly and violently I had to yank my hand away.

As I stared at her, trying to process what I'd just felt, she glanced over at me. "What?"

"Are you sure you're okay?" I asked. Fear, grief, and longing were her foremost feelings. But they also mixed with anger and shame.

"I'm fine," she said. "Did you try to feel my emotions?"

"I was trying to reassure you that everything would be okay, but after what I just felt, I'm worried I don't know how bad they might actually be."

Harriet huffed, then stood. "I don't need to be here. I'll wait for you with Mona."

She was gone before I could ask her to stay.

Whether it was paranoia or reality, I felt like everyone in the room was staring at me after Harriet walked out. Surely, they didn't know who I was, but they might have recognized Harriet and wondered who she was with.

I felt like sinking in my seat and disappearing, but the last time I'd done that, I'd depleted my magical abilities.

"What are you doing here?" Xander hissed as he slid into the seat next to me. "I cannot believe she brought you here."

I was just as shocked to see him as he seemed to be seeing me. "What are *you* doing here?" I asked. "Monroe was my cousin. I thought I'd pay my respects."

Xander looked like his head might explode.

"And where's Laura?" I asked. "I'm sure she won't be happy you're sitting with me."

"I'd never bring Laura to—uh—"

"What?" I looked around. "A magical funeral? There seem to be lots of non-magical people here."

"You need to leave. Now." Xander sounded angry and worried, but the stubbornness inside me didn't care how angry or worried he was.

"I'm not leaving," I said. "I have to be here."

"To pay respects to a man who was trying to kill you?" Xander hissed.

A couple of people in front of us turned around but then seemed to think better of it.

"How do you know he was trying to kill me? He had plenty of chances with us being in the same Mayor for a Day race."

"He was biding his time," Xander said. "He couldn't just do it out in the open. Why else would he have been there? He didn't care about taxes. He knew he wouldn't win."

"If you knew he was going to try to kill me, why wouldn't you have warned me?" I asked. "I thought we were friends."

"Can we discuss this somewhere else?"

"No," I said. "The service is starting."

Xander sat back in the chair as we watched Renée walk out to address the crowd.

"Renée?" I asked Xander.

He pressed a finger to his lips, silencing me.

When I looked back up at the stage, Renée was staring right at me with a concerned look on her face. Her gaze shifted to my left—to Xander.

I noticed Xander shrink a bit out of the corner of my eye as Renée gave him a withering glare.

"I'd like to thank you all for coming today," she said. "Monroe was a pillar of the community and will be missed."

I turned to look at Xander, who shook his head almost imperceptibly.

How could he be sitting there like this was no big deal? If Monroe had been trying to kill me, why was Renée up there singing his praises?

"As a member of the Magical Governing Council, Monroe made many improvements to the well-being of the magical community."

My mouth fell open. Monroe was one of the magical council members? Like the magical council that rules over the Grand Witch of the States? The magical council that would rule over me if I accepted the position?

I nearly vomited. My hair was definitely changing color, not that anyone around me was likely surprised since they all knew magic existed.

"Monroe was not much of a family man," Renée continued and smiled when the crowd chuckled. "But his adopted mother was easily the most important person in his life. Darla would like to say a few words now."

Renée walked off the stage, and the woman who had nominated Deacon—Monroe—for Mayor for a Day took her place. Darla wore a bright, multi-colored dress, complete with a colorful top hat. The tears that flowed down her face starkly contrasted the cheerful colors.

"From the moment he was born, I knew Monroe was special." She read from a sheet of paper, her eyes never lifting to look at the crowd, her fingers tight around the podium's ledge.

She spoke about Monroe's accomplishments from the

time he could walk until his death. With each one, I grew angrier and angrier.

This man had killed his own mother, his aunt, and had done who knows what to my own mom. Tears welled in my eyes at the realization that my mom—Emily—hadn't returned. Even with him gone, she was still missing.

A tug in my navel told me I needed to revisit the mural, but I couldn't just leave the funeral. Plus, I was here for a purpose. I had to see if anyone acted suspiciously.

Darla cleared her throat, and I glanced up to see her staring at me. "I'm well aware that my Monroe was murdered. To the person responsible, you'll get what's coming to you."

Every eye turned to look at me—the person Darla thought was responsible for Monroe's murder.

"She didn't do it," a woman's voice boomed from the back of the auditorium. "I did."

Everyone turned to see who had said it, but it was impossible to make out the face in the shadows.

I glanced back at Darla, who was now staring into the darkness behind me. "I'll kill you if it's the last thing I do."

Chaos erupted around me.

Xander grabbed my arm and pulled me onto the aisle floor. The carpet was rough, burning my elbows as he tugged on me.

"Stop," I said. But there's no way he could have heard me over the surrounding cacophony.

He tugged more, and I wiggled my way behind him as we made our way toward the stage.

Darla was no longer there—Renée stood in her place.

She raised her hands above her head, and the place went silent.

I tried to speak, but the words wouldn't come out of my mouth.

Xander shook his head at me.

He had a lot of explaining to do. Well, either him or Renée or Lucy or Harriet or someone. I was tired of being in the dark about everything.

24

Renée smiled from the stage. "Now that we're all quiet let me make one thing very clear: no one is going to kill anyone. We do not murder one another. And whoever was in the back of the room admitting to doing so will be held accountable for their actions."

Not being able to speak was one of the weirdest feelings in the world. I could breathe and think, but whenever I tried to make a sound, it wouldn't come out. It's like when you're in a nightmare, and you can't scream. Only not quite as terrifying.

"Now, I will release you in a moment, but when I do, we are going to continue with the funeral as planned. If you must speak or attend to anything, please do so away from here." Renée dropped her hands, and murmurs rippled through the auditorium. "If you wish to stay, please return to your seats." She looked down at Xander and me. "If you wish to leave, you may do so now."

Renée's evil eye was terrifying, but I wasn't backing down. Not anymore.

I brushed off Xander's grip, stood, and returned to my seat. Xander followed and sat next to me with a huff.

Renée seemed surprised but regained her composure quickly. "We'll begin the personal accounts. The microphone is open for whoever would like to speak."

A line formed down the aisle next to Xander.

"Switch me places," I said.

Xander looked at me like I was insane.

"Now," I said. "Switch me."

I stood and started pushing him over.

"Fine, stop," Xander said, plopping into my old seat while I took his. "Why do you want that seat? You didn't seem ready to leave."

"I'm not leaving," I said. "I'm watching."

The people lining up to speak had one thing in common—they were all women.

As I watched them make their way to the stage, most of them seemed to be sad. I needed to find the one who wasn't. Or at least the one faking it.

I made myself as big as possible, jutting my elbow out into the aisle.

The first woman spoke on stage about how she'd dated Monroe when they were in high school.

Someone walked past me, accidentally bumping my elbow. The contact was enough to get a slight read on her emotions—sad. Deeply sad.

"Sorry," she said, glancing down with tears in her eyes, then continuing up the aisle.

The next four who touched my elbow were all just as distraught.

Did they not know how terrible this man was?

As woman after woman spoke about how much she loved Monroe, I was starting to doubt my knowledge of him. Perhaps Neve and Harriet and Xander were wrong. Maybe he wasn't my cousin. Maybe he was just a prominent member of the magical community like Renée had said.

But if that was the case, why was Xander so eager to get me out of there, and why had Darla all but accused me of killing Monroe?

Another woman bumped my elbow, but this one wasn't sad. She was nervous and maybe even a bit excited.

I glanced up, but the woman's face was covered in a bright pink lacy veil.

She didn't look down at me but took her handkerchief under the veil and dabbed at her eyes.

When her hands came back down, the handkerchief was completely clean. Not a single discoloration where a tear might have been.

This was the woman I was looking for.

Before I knew what I was doing, I stood and joined the line behind her. She wore a bright pink dress that matched her veil, gloves, and pillbox hat on top of her shiny black hair fastened into a low bun.

"What are you doing?" Xander hissed beside me.

I ignored him. I needed to see who this woman was.

Magical energy buzzed around me like I hadn't felt before. I'd never been in the presence of so many magical people.

As she took a step, she dropped her handkerchief on the floor. This was my opportunity.

I snatched it up and quickly examined it—still perfectly clean and dry with a monogram in the top corner with the letters O.B.

I tapped her on the shoulder.

She turned and flashed a pair of piercing green eyes at me from beneath the veil. "Yes?" She sniffled, but it was thoroughly unconvincing.

"I think you dropped this," I said, handing her the handkerchief.

"How clumsy of me." Her voice was super high-pitched. "I can hardly feel anything with these gloves on." She pulled the glove off her right hand and took the handkerchief. Bruises covered her forearm.

I glanced up at her. "Are you okay?"

She yanked the glove back on.

"I don't know what you're talking about," she said. "I'm perfectly fine."

"But those bruises—"

She stepped closer to me. "Are nothing." She turned away from me.

Woman after woman made their way up to the microphone, each of them speaking with fondness of Monroe.

"Did you know him?" I asked the woman.

She didn't respond.

We edged closer to the stage.

Maybe she hadn't heard me.

I tapped her shoulder, and she whipped around to look at me. "Would I be in this line if I didn't know him?"

"Did you date him?"

She let out a burst of laughter, then glanced around to check that no one was witnessing our exchange.

"Not in a million years," she said. "Did *you* know Monroe?"

"Not really."

"It shows." She turned away from me and marched up the steps to the stage.

I hadn't seen it before, but the casket was open for viewing at the top of the steps.

The woman stopped and looked inside, dropping something where I guessed Monroe's head would have been.

I hurried behind her to look inside, but the only thing I saw was the dead man I only knew as Deacon in way too much makeup. Whatever she had dropped must have been tiny.

I tried to take a closer look, but a woman behind me tapped me on the shoulder and said, "You've had enough time with him. It's my turn."

The woman in pink stood behind the microphone. Her high-pitched voice rang through the building, loud and clear. "Monroe was a horrible man. He deserved to die."

The crowd gasped as she darted off stage.

I tried to go after her, but someone caught me by the arm and dragged me back behind the coffin and off the stage.

Renée.

"What in the world do you think you're doing?" she asked.

"I was trying to catch Monroe's killer," I said. "But now she's gone."

"You think she killed Monroe?" Renée looked behind me. "She's part of an incredibly well-to-do family in the magical community."

"She just said he deserved to die."

"He *did* deserve to die."

"Then why are you up there talking about how wonderful he was?" I recognized I sounded like a pathetic child whining about why she wasn't allowed to buy a piece of candy from the checkout aisle. I cleared my throat. "I have so many questions about today."

"Of that, I'm certain," Renée said. "But I don't have time to answer them now. I need to attend to the funeral. And I need you to leave."

"Why?"

"I don't have time for this."

"Then I'm not leaving."

"Fine," she said, peeking behind me again. "But stay with Xander."

"I would, but it's kind of awkward with him and Laura and—"

"I don't care if it's awkward. He is your guardian. You will stay with him."

My jaw dropped open. "My what?"

Renée closed her eyes and took a deep breath before opening them again. "I will explain everything when the funeral is over. But right now, I need you to—"

She didn't get the rest of her sentence out before an explosion from the other side of the curtain drowned her out.

The blast threw me back into the wall, sending pain down my spine. Renée landed on top of me and got to her feet relatively quickly.

She held a hand out for me, but I couldn't imagine getting up.

Renée knelt beside me. "May I?"

I nodded. "Please."

She put her palms on my bare arms. Almost instantly, I felt better. She and I both had healing powers, but this was the first time I'd been on the receiving end. Well, other than when my ghostly grandmother had healed my broken ankle in a dream—or what I'd thought was a dream.

"Thank you," I said, this time taking her hand to come to a stand.

Renée hurried away to see what had happened. I didn't have to follow to know that whatever the lady in pink had put in the casket had blown up what was left of Monroe's body.

My assumptions were confirmed as I hurried to see Renée use her magic to extinguish the flames climbing the curtains behind what was left of the casket. "Who would have done this?"

Screams filled the auditorium as the sound of feet trampled out of the building.

"The lady in pink," I said. "She dropped something in his casket. It must have been a bomb."

Xander practically leaped onto the stage and pulled me into a big bear hug. "Are you okay? I didn't see you get on the stage. I thought maybe—"

I pulled away. "Maybe what? That you'd get in trouble for not being a very good guardian? I'd guess letting your—" I waved my arms in the air trying to figure out what the heck I'd be called in this situation. "—whatever I am get blown up would basically mean you're fired, right?"

"It'd be much worse than that if you got blown up," Renée said.

He didn't look away from me. "How did you know?"

"I may have let it slip," Renée said, wiping soot from her hands onto her orange and yellow jumper. "But if you had been doing your job properly, Ellie would never have been here in the first place."

Xander looked torn between our death stares.

"How about this," I said. "You're fired. I don't need a guardian."

I walked away before he could refute it . . . and before he could see the tears rolling down my cheeks.

Once I made it out to the lobby, I searched for the woman in pink.

Not only was she not in the lobby, no one was. Everyone had left.

So much for me figuring out who killed Monroe.

I sighed and walked outside to find Mona parked near the entrance, waiting for me.

"What happened in there?"

"A lady in pink blew up Monroe's dead body, and I found out Xander is my guardian."

I sucked in a breath. Xander told me he'd never lie to me. I believed him.

"Did you see anything out here?" I asked, steadying my voice.

"Only a massive crowd practically falling all over themselves to get out of there," Harriet said.

"I guess this was a wasted trip," I said. "I'm sorry I made you come."

Harriet shrugged and looked out the window.

I tickled Mona's dash. "Let's go home."

Mona roared to life and started on her magic-fueled drive back to the house.

I pulled out my phone to find no less than twenty text messages from Xander, five from Renée, and one from Jake.

I didn't even open Xander's or Renée's. Jake's said —*call me.*

He answered on the first ring, "Hello? Ellie? Are you okay?"

"I'm fine," I said. "Just heading home from the funeral."

"The one where the corpse was blown to smithereens?"

"That's the one," I said, trying not to laugh. "How did you know?"

"Georgia told me. She was there."

"It seems everyone in the magical community was," I said. "He was some sort of politician."

"Is that so?"

"And I caught wind that they think someone magical did it," I said. "I guess it's too late now, but maybe for future cases, we should have a magical coroner on standby."

"About that," Jake said. "We think we know who's responsible for the murders."

"You do?" I asked, switching my phone to my ear opposite Harriet.

"I didn't want to be the one to tell you this, but it only makes sense, especially if it was a magical murder."

My throat constricted. What was he getting at?

When I didn't say anything, he continued, "Harriet killed them, Ellie. I'm so sorry."

I did my best to stay as calm as I could. "Really?" I choked out. "Are you sure?"

Harriet glanced over at me with a questioning stare.

I shrugged.

"We're certain," Jake said. "Because Deacon was such an important person—er—warlock in the magical community, the magical investigation team insisted on being part of the case."

I tried to keep my feelings in check. I didn't need my hair giving me away.

"I'm sorry I didn't tell you," Jake said as if sensing my irritation. "They told me not to involve you since you were so close to Harriet and since Monroe was your cousin."

"You knew he was my cousin?" I asked. "This whole time?"

"Not the whole time," Jake said. "But, yes, I knew."

Harriet was still staring at me, but I didn't look at her. I couldn't. Could she have killed Monroe and Susan? She'd told me she was going to, but then she said she didn't do it.

"Do you know where she is?" Jake's voice sounded about a million miles away through the phone.

"Huh?"

"Do you know where Harriet is?"

I glanced out my window. "No."

"Are you sure?"

"She went with me to the funeral, but she left before it was over."

"Do you think she blew up the casket to get rid of any additional evidence?"

My stomach tightened. "She had already left when it blew up."

"How about we talk about this in person?" Jake asked. "I can bring dinner over to your house, and you can tell me what you saw at the funeral."

"No," I said too quickly. "I mean, I didn't see anything."

"You didn't? But isn't that why you went?"

Jake was practically interrogating me over the phone. "Why don't you ask Georgia? She was there. Or maybe Xander? Or this mystery team you've been working with behind my back?"

"Ellie, I didn't mean to—"

"I'm about done with people lying to me," I said, pent-up feelings pouring out of me. "First Xander and Renée, now you. Maybe Harriet. I just can't deal with it anymore. I don't want to have anything to do with this case. Okay? I'm done."

I hung up the phone before he could try to talk me into helping him.

I tickled Mona's dash and said, "Take us somewhere safe."

Mona drove at lightning speed as Harriet and I sat in silence.

"They think I killed Monroe, don't they?" Harriet finally said.

"It doesn't matter what they think," I said. "I know the truth."

"It would only make sense they'd think it was me," Harriet said. "But I assure you, it wasn't."

When we pulled into Cliff Hallow and slowed near Lucy's, I groaned. "I do not want to go to Lucy's," I said to Mona, tickling the dash.

"I don't think she brought us here to take us to Lucy's," Harriet said. "Look."

Harriet pointed at her house, where a seemingly ordinary car was parked in the driveway.

"Is that your car?" I asked. It hadn't been in the driveway when I'd picked her up.

"I don't have a car yet," she said. "That would be a magical officer. They're in my house."

Mona sped up as we passed Harriet's house and out of town.

"If you didn't do it, then they won't find anything," I said. "It's probably good they're in there looking around, don't you think?"

Harriet didn't reply.

Mona drove for what felt like hours. I could have stopped her—told her we had gone far enough—but I was too tired. I'd spent my entire life trying to figure out who to trust. I thought I'd gotten pretty good at judging character, but apparently, I hadn't.

Xander was my guardian. *Guardian.*

That's why he showed up out of nowhere.

That's why he was so protective of me.

That's why Bernardo said it wouldn't work between Xander and me.

I felt so stupid.

Eventually, Mona slowed to a stop, pulling into my empty driveway. "You were just waiting for the house to be empty, weren't you?" I smiled. At least I could trust Mona. And Penelope.

Harriet immediately jumped out of the passenger seat and ran inside.

When I walked in, Penelope oinked up at me.

I gathered her up in my arms. "You knew about Xander, didn't you? That's why you didn't want us to kiss."

Penelope let out the tiniest oink I'd ever heard, confirming what I'd just said.

"Thank you," I said. "Next time, I'll listen to you."

Wix came charging down the stairs with Harriet hot

on his heels. When he reached the front door, he started barking so loudly I thought my eardrums might burst.

When the doorbell rang, I knew it was him.

Penelope grumbled in my arms.

"Wix, hush," Harriet said, and Wix stopped.

"Ellie, I know you don't want to talk to me," Xander yelled from the other side of the door. "But I can explain everything."

"There's nothing to explain," I said. "You were just doing your job hanging out with me, and now you don't have to anymore. I'm sure Laura will be thrilled."

Before Xander could say anything else, I walked upstairs and closed myself and Penelope in our bedroom.

When I woke, my eyes were puffy from crying.

I pulled on a hoodie and some flip-flops and snuck out of the house, leaving Penelope asleep in her little bed next to mine.

It was still mostly dark outside, but the sky was warming with the sun's approach. The barn was just as I'd left it when I'd been there with Andrea.

At the thought of her, my stomach twisted a bit. Where was she? Was she the one who had stood in the back of the auditorium at the funeral confessing to the murders? Or could that have been Harriet?

I shook my head. I wasn't dealing with the case anymore.

I pulled the curtain back and sat on the sofa facing the mural. It was still daytime, and the diner was the prime focus. No faces were turned my way, peeking out the window. No lights flickered. No specks of magic appeared.

My heart felt as empty as my stomach.

"Why is this happening?" I asked. Who I was talking to, I didn't know. "How did I misread Xander's cues? How could he have acted like he liked me when he was my guardian?"

"Why can't both things be true?" a whisper said next to me.

When I turned, Esme sat—or rather, hovered—on the couch next to me.

"Can you see me?" she asked.

"Yes," I said.

Her eyes went wide. Iridescent tears trickled down her opaque cheeks. "I hoped your magic would grow enough for you to see me."

She wrapped her arms around my neck, and I shivered. It didn't feel like a normal hug. There was a bit of weight to it and a lot of cold, but it was nice feeling her touch either way.

I circled my arms around her and hugged her back, the tears on the side of my face closest to her freezing on the way down my cheek.

Esme let go just before my teeth started chattering.

"How are you here?" I asked, still shocked that my dead grandmother was right next to me.

"I decided to stay back, hoping either you or your mother would make your way back here," she said. "I'm so happy you did."

"Do you know if Emily is still alive?" I asked.

She shook her head. "I wish I did. But my presence

and knowledge only extend to the property line. It's both a blessing and a curse, but this is where I will spend my eternity."

I had so many questions. "Did you see Ty murder his uncle?"

She nodded. "If only you could have seen me then, I would have shown you right to the evidence. Thankfully, Penelope was there."

I thought back to when we'd been in the cornfield and Penelope had freaked out during the first investigation I'd gotten myself into. She'd practically led me to the body.

"Has Penelope always been able to see you?"

She smiled. "She has."

"What about other ghosts?" I asked. "Can Penelope see them too?"

"I would suspect she can," Esme said. "But let's talk about Xander for a moment, shall we?"

My heart dropped.

"I can sense you're hurting." Esme put an icy hand on my arm.

"He lied to me," I said. "He said he'd never lie to me, and he did."

"It was not his choice to do so."

"He could have stayed away from me, though, guarded me from afar. Or been horrible or something. I thought we were friends."

"I believe if you asked Xander, he would say you are friends. Perhaps even more than friends."

"He's dating Laura."

"I gathered as much." Esme shook her head. "It's

baffling to me. Laura and her family have always been so against magic until Xander showed up."

"I fired him," I said. "I told him I didn't want him to be my guardian anymore."

She pursed her lips. It was hard to tell what she was thinking with the vapor-like quality of her face. The harder I tried to focus on her, the more out of focus she became.

"I believe that can be undone if you so choose," she said. "Have they assigned you another guardian?"

"I don't want a guardian," I said. "I don't want to be Grand Witch of the States."

Esme didn't flinch or gasp like Lucy and Renée did when I said it. She simply nodded. "I completely understand your hesitancy. Especially with the life you've probably had. I can't even imagine. I'm so sorry I didn't find you sooner."

"How did you find out about me? Was it Xander who told you?"

She nodded. "He showed up out of the blue one day and let me know I had a granddaughter."

"How did he know?"

"I think that's something you need to take up with him," she said. "I may be here, but I cannot give you all the answers you're looking for, even if I wanted to."

Frustration crawled up my spine. "Do you know who my father is?"

"I assumed it was Jake, but he told me over and over again it couldn't be him." Esme shrugged. "Though you do look like him a bit, right around the eyes."

I smiled. "Is there any way he might have just

forgotten—uh—you know?" I could feel the heat rising up my neck just thinking about Jake and Emily being intimate.

"It is rare magic to be able to erase a single occurrence in someone's memory completely. It is far easier to erase bigger portions, but the fact that he still remembers Emily and their time together makes it less likely."

"But possible?" I asked, my hopes rising in my chest.

"With magic, anything is possible," Esme said.

The sound of the door opening startled me. The curtain was pulled so I couldn't see who walked in, but when I looked back, Esme was gone.

The sound of footsteps made their way toward me. "Ellie? Are you in here?" It was Harriet.

"I'm back here," I said.

She peeked around the curtain. "You're up early."

I patted the couch next to me for her to sit. She did.

"Just needed some time to think," I said. "The whole Xander thing is really getting to me."

"When I was here last, I told him he needed to stay emotionally unattached. I think at that point, it was too late. You Vanderwick women attract men like pillows attract Wix."

I laughed. "If only I could attract a decent man. I seem to find all the crappy ones."

"Xander isn't crappy. He's just your guardian—or was."

"Was?"

"Didn't you fire him?"

"Oh right," I said. "I guess I had that authority."

"That's probably why he didn't tell you he was your

guardian. Not growing up with magic, being self-sufficient your entire life, you would have fired him the instant he mentioned guardianship."

She was right. There was no way I would have allowed him to be my guardian—or anyone, for that matter.

"Would *you* allow someone to be your guardian?" I asked.

"If I was in line to become the next Grand Witch of the States? Absolutely, I would. It's tradition."

"Tradition?"

"Every future Grand Witch is assigned one. It's kind of like the Secret Service for the president."

I was starting to feel stupid for firing him. "So, now what? I just don't have one?"

"Oh no, you'll always have one. It just won't be Xander."

"Does that mean that I could date Xander—I mean—if he and Laura broke up?"

She furrowed her brow. "Who said you couldn't date Xander?"

"Bernardo," I said.

"Makes sense." She nodded. "But no. You still can't date him."

"Why not?"

"Have they not told you anything?" She waved a hand around. "Lucy and Renée—I thought they were in charge of your magical training."

"They are," I said. "Lucy mostly because Renée is always so busy. But they haven't told me why I can't date Xander."

"It's just that Xander—"

"That's enough, Harriet," Andrea said from behind us.

Harriet's face turned bright red. "I think she has the right to know."

"That might be true, but you won't be the one to tell her." Andrea strode over to us.

"Where have you been?" I asked.

"Working," Andrea said. "And now, I'm here. I'm your new guardian."

"I didn't realize they'd assign me another guardian so quickly," I said.

"They assigned me to you months ago," Andrea said. "A backup to Xander."

"Were you at the funeral?" I asked.

"Yes," Andrea said. "And before you ask, I was not the one who admitted to killing Monroe. Nor was I the one who blew up the casket."

"Did you kill Monroe?"

"Why don't we go inside and talk to the others," Andrea said, avoiding my question.

"Others?" Harriet asked.

"We thought it would be best to all talk to you at the same time," Andrea said. "That way, we can answer all of your questions."

I glanced at Harriet, and she shrugged.

"Okay, let's go inside," I said.

"I'll stay out here," Harriet said. "And hang out with the mural."

Andrea looked at the wall, and her face paled. "What is that?"

"It's a mural," I said slowly.

"But what's it of?" Andrea took a step toward it, and tingles rushed to my scalp.

I stepped between her and the mural, holding my hands up. "Don't get any closer."

Andrea looked at me and stepped back. "Sorry. I just—well—never mind."

"What?" I asked. "Do you know this place?"

"I'm sorry, I can't say." Andrea turned and walked past the curtain toward the studio door.

I glanced at Harriet, who shrugged, then at the mural. If Andrea knew anything about it, I was going to get answers.

I marched into the house and was greeted by several people sitting around my large dining room table.

The head of the table was open for me. Andrea stood in the doorway.

Around the table were several faces I recognized, as well as a few I didn't. Renée sat to my right with Lucy next to her. My heart caught in my chest when I saw Bernardo and Xander on the other side of Lucy—Xander sitting at the end of the table opposite me.

I smiled at Bernardo, but he simply glanced down at a stack of papers in front of him.

Georgia and then two men—warlocks—I didn't recognize sat on the long side of the table across from Lucy, Renée, and Bernardo.

"I suppose I will begin," Renée said. "Ellie, we've decided now is the time to come clean with everything.

We will answer all the questions we can. In return, we expect you to make a decision about becoming Grand Witch of the States."

My mouth felt like I'd taken a big bite of flour. I couldn't speak. They wanted me to decide? Right now?

"Your decision does not mean you will take over the position right away," Renée said. "However, it does mean you will have to get more serious about developing your magic and becoming immersed in the magical community."

"We don't, however, expect you to decide before we answer your questions," one of the older warlocks I didn't recognize said.

I nodded and tried to hold back the tears pricking at the corners of my eyes.

"Let's go around the table and introduce ourselves," the older warlock said. "I am Lars Templeton, President of the Magical Governing Council."

"Samuel Killroy," the next warlock said. "Magical Council Member."

"Georgia Barnette," Georgia—Jake's fiancée and Xander and Bernardo's cousin—said. "Magical Council Member Elect of the States."

"Bernardo Wix," Bernardo said. "Magical Council Member."

Xander hesitated, then looked up at me with what seemed to be an apology in his eyes. "Xander Wix, Vice President of the Magical Governing Council."

28

I didn't know whether it was Xander's last name—Wix—or the fact that he was Vice President of the Magical Governing Council that made me stare at him long past his introduction.

I barely heard Lucy and Renée introduce themselves.

Wix—Like the dog in the barn with Harriet.

Wix—Like the dealership—Wix and Sons—where I'd purchased Mona.

Wix.

It was a name I'd seen my entire life. Since I could remember.

Trucks with Wix Lighting on the side.

Wix Diner.

The Wix Theater.

Mr. Wix, my seventh-grade English teacher—the only teacher who was ever nice to me.

"Ellie?" Lucy asked. "Are you okay?"

I sucked in a deep breath, trying to steady my

emotions. I'd known Xander's father had sold Mona to me, but I didn't realize he'd owned the dealership.

My hair was probably a rainbow of color on my head. Not only was Xander probably related to all these other Wixes, he was also the Vice President of the Magical Governing Council. Which was probably why we couldn't date. Ever.

Tears stung at my eyes. I cleared my throat. "Shall we get on with the questions and answers?"

Renée nodded once. "But before we begin, I'd like to impose lie prevention if no one is opposed?"

Nods all around the table.

Renée waved her hands in the air. What felt like tape on my tongue made me nearly gag.

"It's not a pleasant sensation," Renée said. "But you need to know that everyone in here will tell you the truth."

"Do any of you know where my mother is?" I asked. "Or if she's dead?"

"We will go around the table and give Ellie our answers," Lars said. "I'll begin. No, I do not know the whereabouts of your mother or whether she is alive or not."

"I do not know where your mother is or if she is dead or alive," Samuel said.

"I believe your mother is alive," Xander said.

My mouth fell open. He thought Emily was alive somewhere and had never told me?

"I am unaware of any—" Bernardo began, but his words halted as if an invisible barrier in his mouth had stopped them.

"Be more specific," Lars said. "You do know some facts about Emily Vanderwick."

"I'm sorry," Bernardo said. "As to your mother's whereabouts or the status of her being alive or dead, I am unaware."

"I do not know where your mother is or whether she is alive or dead," Lucy said. "Sorry, kiddo."

"I also do not know where your mother is or whether she is alive," Renée said. "Do you have any follow-up questions?"

"What gives you reason to believe my mother is alive?" I asked Xander, barely hearing Lucy's and Renée's answers.

"I cannot say," Xander said.

"Wait, you can't just not say," I said. "Isn't that against the rules of what we're here to do?" Anger flowed through me. My hair was likely a bright red at this point.

"You have to know that if I could tell you, I would," Xander said. "That's why I never brought it up before."

I was about to refute him when Lars held up a hand.

"Xander—and anyone at this table—may hold on to private information if they truly believe it has to stay secret."

"Then what's the point?" I pushed away from the table and came to a stand. "If he can just sit over there keeping all his secrets? What else will you hold on to?"

"Ellie, please sit down," Renée said. "We have a lot of information for you."

Reluctantly, I sat back down, my curiosity outweighing my frustration.

"Thank you," Lars said. "Now, what other questions do you have for us?"

"If there's reason to believe my mother is still alive somewhere, why aren't you focusing on finding her and making her Grand Witch of the States?" I asked.

"We have been searching for your mother for years," Samuel said. "But every tip we get leads us astray. If she is alive, we believe your mother doesn't want to be found."

Xander shifted in his seat but said nothing.

"If we do find her, would she automatically become Grand Witch?" I asked.

"Not if you've already been sworn in—and possibly even before that," Lars said. "There's some concern about her disappearance. If she disappeared willingly, we would guess she doesn't want to be Grand Witch, especially with how thoroughly she has done so."

"And now that Monroe is deceased, there's no reason to believe she's being held against her will anymore," Bernardo said, an apologetic look spread over his face both when he glanced at Xander and then at me. "He would have been the only one with reason to hold her."

"Which would mean she's either dead or not coming back," I said, trying to keep my words from shaking as they exited my mouth.

Lars nodded.

Georgia looked down into her lap and brushed a tear from her eye.

I cleared my throat, trying to keep my emotions in check.

"Ellie, have you learned to control your hair?" Xander asked.

I shifted my gaze to him. "Why?"

"I've noticed it a couple of times now, but your hair almost seems to glitch at times. Like you're actually in control of it."

I pulled a few strands toward me. I would have expected them to be red or blue or something, but they were white like usual. "I-I don't know," I said, my heart racing in my chest. "I felt tingles on my scalp like normal. Has my hair changed at all since I've been here?"

All the heads shook from side to side.

"No? It hasn't changed?" I was starting to panic. Or was that panic actually excitement? Could I control my emotions enough to control my hair?

"It seems your magic is catching up nicely," Lars said. "You've done a good job with her, Lucy."

Lucy blushed. "She's been a model student."

"But I've only just gotten the hang of lighting candles," I said. "That's, like, the easiest thing in the world to do."

Lucy smirked. "I only told you it was the easiest thing. Strangely enough, fire is one of the hardest magics to learn."

Bernardo beamed at me. I couldn't help but smile back. Had my magic really progressed that much by simply working on lighting a few candles?

"It seems you're a natural when it comes to your magic. You just needed the confidence to perform," Renée explained. "When you did your disappearing act, we realized your magic was stronger than we thought possible."

"I'm happy to hear that," I said. "But can we go back to something for a minute?"

Renée nodded.

"Why did you allow Monroe to be on the Magical Governing Council if you knew he was a criminal?"

Lars sucked in a breath and exhaled slowly. "The Magical Governing Council is a lifetime position—similar to the Grand Witch. And used to be elected as young as sixteen years old."

"You allow sixteen-year-olds to be on the magical council?" I gaped at him.

"We did," he said. "Esme was very against the idea. With her guidance, we've changed a great number of the rules—now women can be on the council, council members have to be over the age of thirty, and your family status within the magical world doesn't matter."

Bernardo and Xander shot each other knowing glances.

"Okay, so what? Once you're on the council, you can't get voted off?" I asked. "Even if you're a criminal?"

"Monroe was very good at covering his tracks," Samuel said. "We could never actually pin anything on him."

"Couldn't you just put this lie detector spell on him?" I asked.

"It's complicated," Renée said. "The council members don't meet very often, and even when they do, it's not always all of them. Monroe has been out of the loop for quite a long time."

"Do you know who killed him?" I asked.

"We have our suspicions, but we've been in contact with the local authorities and the magical authorities," Samuel said.

"Who did it?" I asked. "Was it Harriet?"

Harriet—who was presumably still out in the barn with Wix—would likely have been arrested already if so, but I had to ask.

"No, it was not Harriet," Samuel said. "However, we can't discuss our suspicions at the moment."

I wasn't involved in the case, but I still wanted to help. "There was green glitter on the tie," I said. "Laura's poster was covered in green glitter."

"They were killed magically," Xander said. "Laura couldn't have done it."

I sighed. He was right. "Andrea had glitter in her purse."

Everyone turned to look at Andrea.

"The glitter was everywhere," Andrea said with a shrug. "It could have been anyone. I didn't kill them."

"But there were only four magical people there—you, me, Monroe, and Coral." I turned back to Samuel. "Have you looked into Coral?"

"We have," Samuel said.

"Is she working with you, too?" I asked.

"No," Samuel said.

"The minute Monroe came to town, I was tasked with following him," Andrea said. "Which wasn't hard since he took a liking to my best friend. He didn't know I was a witch."

"I knew you were a witch," I said. "How do you know Monroe didn't?"

"He was very suspicious of other witches and warlocks. If he'd have noticed my magic, he would have bolted," Andrea said. "His magic may have been strong once, but it wasn't as attuned as yours. You've been working on your magic daily for months. His was slightly out of shape, just like when someone doesn't exercise for long periods of time."

"How did he conceal his magic from me?" I asked.

The table was silent for a moment. Bernardo snuck a glance at Xander, but Xander didn't say anything.

"Xander, do you know?" I asked.

Xander shot an irritated glance at Bernardo. "I have my suspicions."

"And they are?" I asked.

"There are witches and warlocks who can hide others' magical trails," Xander said. "It's illegal magic, but it is possible."

"Monroe was trying to stay under the radar," Samuel said. "Meaning he didn't use his magic unless absolutely necessary. That also helped keep it masked."

"If you were supposed to be staying close to him," I asked Andrea, "why weren't you there when he and Susan were killed?"

"I was on a phone call," Andrea said.

"Who was protecting me at that point?" I asked.

"Laura was with you," Xander said. "When I saw you alone outside, I asked her to join you for lunch."

"I'm sure that made her happy," I said.

Xander didn't reply.

"And you're certain Harriet didn't kill Monroe?" I asked. "Because the police—Jake—seemed pretty sure she was responsible."

"They found some evidence in her new home that suggested she might have been the one who shot Monroe —bullets and such—but the magic didn't match up. From everything we can tell, Harriet is innocent and will not be taken into custody." Samuel didn't smile. He was so serious.

I, on the other hand, was elated to know my cousin hadn't killed anyone.

29

As if on cue, Harriet came through the back door with Wix.

Everyone turned to look as she walked past the door to the dining room and began up the stairs.

"Harriet, will you come in here a moment?" Renée asked.

Harriet's footsteps returned to the doorway, where Andrea moved to allow her to enter.

"We wanted to let you know you are off the hook for Monroe's murder," Renée said. "You can return to your home whenever you choose."

Harriet reached down to pet Wix and said, "I'll stay until Ellie can take me home."

Renée nodded, and Harriet turned to leave.

"I knew you didn't do it," I said.

Harriet turned back and smiled at me. "Thanks."

"Do you have any additional questions?" Lars asked.

"Only about a thousand," I said. "But I'm afraid we're running out of time."

"What do you mean?" Lars asked.

"I have to be at the Strawberry Festival opening cere-monies in less than an hour," I said. "I *am* one of the last two Mayor for a Day candidates, after all."

I silently prayed the stalling tactic would work.

Lars looked around the table, each person giving him a slight nod before looking back at me. "So be it. We can answer questions again after the festival concludes this evening. At that time, we will need your answer about whether you will accept the Grand Witch position."

"Oh, I do have one more question," I said, looking at Xander. "How did you know where I was?"

He shifted in his seat. "What do you mean?"

"When you told Esme where I was, how did you know where to find me?"

Every head turned to look at Xander.

Xander cleared his throat. He seemed just as nervous as I was. "I received intel that Emily may have had a baby before she went missing."

"From who?" Lars asked.

"I'm sorry," Xander said. "I can't tell you that."

"Was it Harriet? Or her mother before she died?" I asked.

Xander shook his head. "I never met Harriet's mother. I wasn't very old myself when Harriet's mother died."

"When did you find out?" I asked.

"Only a few days before I told your grandmother," Xander said. "She didn't ask where I got the information. How did you know I was the one who told her about you?"

"She told me," I said. "I can see her ghost sometimes. We talked about it this morning."

Lars gaped at me. In fact, the entire table gaped at me.

"Is that strange?" I asked, then looked at Xander. "You told me ghosts were real."

"They are real," Xander said slowly.

"It's just that ghosts rarely interact with us," Georgia explained. "They can protect and guide us, but they don't usually show themselves."

"I don't know that Esme meant to show herself," I said. "She was surprised I could see her."

Lucy's mouth twitched up in a smile. "I told you," she said to no one and everyone.

"You certainly did," Renée said. "You certainly did."

"Told them what?" I asked.

"Only that you are one of the most powerful witches I've ever encountered," Lucy said.

My phone rang from the counter where it was plugged in.

"Why don't you get that," Georgia said. "It's Jake. I know he'd love to talk to you."

I still wasn't a huge Georgia fan—I wanted Jake single in case my mother ever returned—but I stood and went to the kitchen to answer the phone.

"Hello?" I said.

"Ellie?" Jake's voice was scratchy. "Are you okay?"

"I'm okay," I said. "It's been quite the morning."

"Georgia said it would be."

I glanced back at the dining room. Everyone sat in silence, waiting for me to return.

"I'm sorry, Ellie," Jake said. "I didn't want to keep you

in the dark about the case, but once I found out he was your cousin and that Harriet might have been responsible, I felt the overwhelming urge to protect you from it. Plus, I didn't want your judgment to be clouded."

"I understand," I said.

"Does that mean you'll help with the next case?"

I smiled to myself. "Of course."

He let out a sigh of relief. "Fantastic. Thank you."

"I should probably get back to my meeting so I'm not late for the festival."

"I'll see you there," he said. "Good luck today. I'm voting for you."

We disconnected the call, and I returned to the dining room.

"Shall we reconvene after today's events?" Lars asked before I took my seat.

"That's probably for the best," I said. "Thank you for answering my questions."

"It's our pleasure," Lars said. "Renée, please remove our tongue ties?"

She waved a hand, and my tongue felt free again. I'd almost forgotten what that felt like.

"It's unpleasant but necessary, so you know we aren't lying to you." Lars stood.

"You're welcome to stay here today if you'd like. Or come to the festival," I said.

"That's very kind of you," Lars said. "I know a few of us have business to attend to."

Samuel and Renée nodded.

I felt awkward standing there as everyone gathered

their belongings. "I should probably go get ready." I turned toward the staircase and started out of the room.

"Ellie?" two voices said in unison.

I turned back in time to see both Xander and Bernardo take a step toward me.

They looked at one another and laughed.

"You go ahead," Bernardo said. "I am sure you have to get back to Laura."

Xander's smile faltered as he followed me out of the room into the entryway.

"I'm so sorry I lied to you, El," he said, shoving his hands deep into his pockets.

"You said you would never lie to me," I said. "How can I trust anything you say ever again?"

"I don't know," Xander said. "I guess it'll take time. I'll prove it to you."

"If you find my mom, will you bring her back to me?" I asked.

"When I find Emily, that's the first thing I'll do."

"You promise?"

"I swear."

"Okay, my turn," Bernardo said, stepping between Xander and me and lifting me into a big hug. "I've waited long enough to see Mi Amor."

I giggled as he kissed my neck.

Over his shoulder, I saw Xander frown and walk out the door.

30

I hurried to put on the clothes Katie had set out for me to wear—a pretty white dress with sensible heels and little strawberry earrings. I pulled my hair up into a French twist, leaving a few spirals hanging down. It was still its usual white, but I didn't have time to think about what that meant.

Bernardo, Harriet, Penelope, Wix, and Andrea waited in silence for me.

"Ready?" I asked, propelling them into motion.

We piled into Mona, Bernardo in front with Penelope on his lap. Harriet sat as far away from Andrea as was physically possible, placing Wix between the two of them.

"I'm sorry I didn't tell you I was on the council," Bernardo said, taking my hand in his. "I couldn't tell you until Lars approved."

I smiled. "It's okay. At least you didn't lie to me about my mother."

"Not that I'm defending him, but if he's not telling you, it must be for a good reason."

I sucked in a breath. "Let's not talk about it, okay?"

Bernardo squeezed my hand.

I parked Mona where Katie had instructed—just behind the town hall. "Thanks for looking out for me," I said to her once everyone else was out of the van. "And for being my friend."

Her steering wheel warmed beneath my fingertips.

"I guess this is it," I said as I joined my friends on the sidewalk overlooking the square.

It was like Strawberry Heaven. A tower of shortcakes stood tall in the center of town with tables circling it. There were about a hundred pieces of shortcake on each table, free for event attendees.

Strawberry decorations hung from every streetlight, someone had temporarily painted the benches red with little black specks, and carnival rides flanked the square on two sides.

"This is amazing," Bernardo said. "Xander said Laura had an eye for decorating, but wow!"

My heart twisted in my chest. Why did I care so much about Xander when Bernardo was right here? Xander was with Laura. Jake was with Georgia. And I was with Bernardo. That's just the way it was.

But my heart wasn't in agreement with any of those three statements. The revelation hit me like a ton of bricks. I glanced over at the gorgeous man next to me. Why couldn't I have the same feelings for him as I did for Xander? They were both gorgeous, intelligent, and warm. If I ever met their mothers, I'd have to tell them how good a job they did with these men.

A pang of memory hit me. Except Xander had lied to

me. Actually, they both had, but Xander's had been worse. Especially after he said he'd never lie to me.

"Ellie? Are you okay?" Bernardo's voice jarred me from my thoughts.

"I am." I pushed my shoulders back. "Let's get to the main stage."

We made our way through the growing crowd.

Coral and Laura stood huddled together talking on stage while Xander and Nick hung out off to the side, looking bored.

"Are you ready?" Coral asked when she saw me, excitement in her voice.

"I'm ready," I said, then turned to Laura. "May the best woman win."

"Mmm-hmm," Laura muttered, reaching over and grabbing Xander's hand.

I wanted to punch her in the face.

Xander glanced at her and said, "Be nice."

She glared at him but didn't say anything else.

I looked away when he turned his attention on me. I didn't need his distraction right now. People would start voting any time now. If they saw me on stage glowering about, they might decide to vote for Laura.

I reached down and picked up Penelope, snuggling into her. "I love you."

She oinked quietly up at me and wiggled her nose.

Nick stepped up to the microphone at the center of the stage. "I'd like to welcome everyone to the Cliff Haven Strawberry Festival."

Cheers came from the crowd. It seemed like the entire town had shown up. Katie and the gang stood off to my left and Harriet and Wix to my right. Bernardo and Xander walked off the stage to join Jake and Georgia out in the center of the crowd.

I didn't let the tightening in my stomach change the smile on my face.

I glanced up at the ringlet of hair hanging down my cheek—still white.

"We have carnival rides, a strawberry shortcake tower, free shortcake and decorating, a petting zoo, and much more." Nick's voice boomed out over the crowd. "But before you head off to take part in the festivities, please head to one of the polling stations and vote for your Cliff Haven Mayor for a Day. The two candidates stand before you—Ellie Vanderwick and Laura Lancaster.

"Ellie has proposed we use some of the town budget to get trash cans and removal for the town square. Laura has proposed we use some of the town budget for updated town decorations." He smiled at each of us. "Either way, your vote will make the town of Cliff Haven a more beautiful place to live. If that's even possible."

The crowd laughed.

"Without further ado, I announce the Cliff Haven Strawberry Festival has begun!"

The crowd cheered, then started forming lines at the polling stations as Laura and I stood on stage waving and smiling.

"How long do we need to stand here?" I asked Laura without dropping my smile.

"As long as they're voting, I suppose," Laura muttered.

So we stood. And stood. And stood.

That explained Katie's choice of flats rather than heels.

If I had stood in heels the entire time, my feet would have hurt like crazy.

Nick turned and smiled at us when the last person left the polls.

"Now what?" Laura asked.

"Now we wait," Nick said. "The polls remain open until the end of the day. Then the votes will be tallied. You'll know by tomorrow, and we'll do a formal ceremony announcing the winner."

Laura was the first to leave the stage.

"I'm sorry I've been so hard on you," Nick said as I started to walk away.

I turned back and looked at him. "Why have you been so hard on me? Is it really because of my magic?"

"Your magic? No," Nick said, shaking his head. "Our families have always been at odds. My mother hated Emily. My grandmother hated Esme. So I'm supposed to hate you."

"Supposed to?" I asked.

He smiled and raked his fingers through his hair. "You're kind of hard to hate. For what it's worth, I hope you win."

"Uh, thanks."

"Maybe, if you're free later, we could take a ride on the Ferris wheel together?"

I glanced behind him where Bernardo stood waiting for me.

Nick looked behind him. "Ah, boyfriend?"

"Sort of," I said. "But thanks for the offer."

"The offer stands," Nick said, tickling Penelope behind the ears. "And it can extend to coffee post-event."

I smiled. "Thanks."

Bernardo wrapped an arm around my shoulder when I walked off the stage. "Should we go to the Ferris wheel?"

"Penelope's not much for heights," I said. "Maybe we could check out the shortcake tower? Where is Andrea?"

He corrected course and started in the other direction. "She had some things to deal with. But don't worry, you have plenty of protection." He squeezed my shoulder.

"I'm glad you're here," I said.

"I sense a but in that statement."

I couldn't help the tears that gathered in the corners of my eyes.

Bernardo stopped and turned to look at me straight on, both of his hands on my shoulders. "If you are not happy, you only have to tell me."

That was the problem. I couldn't tell him. I couldn't form the words.

"I am a strong man. I can handle rejection," Bernardo said.

"I'm sorry," I finally managed. "I-I just—"

"You don't feel the same way for me as I feel for you." It was a statement, not a question.

I nodded.

He gathered me up in his arms, Penelope between us. "It is okay. We can be friends."

My tears collected on his shirt, but I couldn't keep them in any longer. Everything felt so messed up. Why couldn't I fall for the gorgeous man who wanted me? Why did I always fall for the bad boys? The ones who cheated. Or lied?

"Can you hold Penelope while I use the restroom to

freshen up?" I asked, wiping away the tears. I didn't want people to see me all worked up. There were still votes to win.

Bernardo took Penelope into his arms, and she snuggled into him.

See? Even Penelope loved him. Ugh.

"I'll be right back."

"Take all the time you need," Bernardo said. "I can wait."

31

The bathroom was empty besides one stall. I stopped in front of the mirror and splashed cold water on my face. I needed to get myself together. People could still be waiting to vote, and if they saw me like this, they'd surely vote for—

Laura.

"Ugh," she said as she walked out of the stall, her gaze meeting mine in the mirror. "We just can't seem to get away from each other, can we?"

"I'm sorry Xander asked you to watch out for me," I said. "I'm sure that wasn't very fun for you."

"You don't have to pretend to be nice to me." Laura started washing her hands, getting far too much soap from the dispenser. "No one's around."

"I'm not pretending," I said. "I just know that must have felt pretty bad to have your boyfriend ask you to look out for another woman."

"The woman he's really in love with?" she asked. "Yeah, it sucks."

I gaped at her. "He's not in love with me."

She rolled her eyes. "Don't act like you don't see it. Why else would he ask me to look out for you?"

"Because I was in danger, and he was my magical guardian," I said. "He had to look out for me. It was his job."

"His job?"

"I guess I'm not the only one he lied to," I said.

She rubbed her hands together furiously, soap bubbles engulfing her fingers.

I checked my makeup in the mirror and started to walk out the door.

"Come back in here," a woman's voice—not Laura's —said.

I turned to find Darla—Monroe's adopted mother— holding Laura with a knife pressed up against her throat.

Laura's hands flung soap everywhere as she flailed around. Her mouth was open, but it was as if she couldn't get the sound out.

"What are you doing?" I asked.

"You killed my boy," Darla said in a ragged voice. "Now, I'm going to kill you."

"I didn't kill him," I said. "I know you think I did. You looked at me at the funeral. But it wasn't me."

"Then who was it?"

"I don't know. I've been trying to figure that out."

"Lies," she said. "You are just trying to save your friend."

Laura wasn't my friend, but I couldn't tell Darla. Regardless of how I felt, I needed to get Laura out safely.

"Why don't you let her go and you can do what you must to me?" I asked.

Laura's mascara streaked down her face with her tears.

I half expected Bernardo to come barging through the door.

"No one is out there to help you," Darla said. "They're too busy doing other things."

"They might not be out there to help me, but if Laura doesn't go back out there soon, Xander Wix will come in looking for her."

Her eyes widened at his name. "But you fired him."

"He's her boyfriend," I said. "And if he finds you holding her here with your magic, he'll likely send you to the same place Monroe is."

Her face crumpled in anger. "Don't you speak his name." She let go of Laura, who promptly bolted out of the bathroom.

I took a step toward the door.

"If you run, I'll kill them all," she said. "Every last person out there."

I considered whether this was a realistic threat, but gauging by her anger level, there was a good chance she'd end up killing at least one person. And the first person she'd encounter when she walked out that door would be Bernardo holding Penelope.

I had to do something. I had to stop her. But I couldn't let her kill me. If she did, I wouldn't be able to protect anyone.

"I'm not running." I held my hands up at shoulder height, showing her my palms. "I swear to you, I did not kill him."

"It wasn't enough to know you'd get all the inheritance? After he did everything for his grandfather—the evil man. Then we find out your trash of a mother had a child."

"Do you know where she is?" I asked. "Did he kill her?"

"She's long gone," Darla said with a smirk. "If Monroe couldn't find her, I doubt she'll ever be found."

Hope landed in my chest. He hadn't killed her. She was simply missing. I could deal with missing.

"I would have given him the inheritance. I didn't care about the money."

"Lies!" she screamed.

I half-expected someone to come barreling in after Laura had gone out, but no one came—not Bernardo, not Lucy, not Xander. I was on my own with a woman teetering on the edge of crazy.

She lunged at me with the knife.

I dodged it, but not fast enough.

It sliced through the skin on my forearm.

More blood than was normal gushed from the wound.

Before I could try to stop the bleeding, she lunged again.

This time, she missed.

"You think you're stronger than me? Smarter?" Darla cackled. "Just because I look like an old witch doesn't mean my magic isn't strong." She pointed the knife tip at me. "See that cut on your forearm? It won't stop bleeding without magical intervention."

I glanced at the door.

"They're not coming. They can't get in. And by the

time they gather their magic together to get through, it'll be too late. Then I'll take them out too. If I'm going down, it won't be without a fight to the death."

I had to act. It was now or never.

I darted toward her and closed my hands around her wrists at the same time I closed my eyes.

I want to be home.

Magic coursed through me with the same sensation as it had the last time.

Darla screamed, but then her screams ended abruptly as we teleported through time and space.

We landed on my kitchen floor with a loud thud.

The knife she'd been holding skidded across the hardwood.

We both watched as it came to rest right in front of the oven.

I reached for it, but she grabbed me by my foot and pulled me back toward her with more strength than a woman of her stature and age would typically have.

She pinned me beneath her and wrapped her hands around my neck.

I grabbed her wrist with both my hands, blood still spilling down my arm. "Get off me. You can't hurt me in this house," I said, hoping the words were true.

"I've already hurt you," Darla said. "You'll bleed out soon enough."

Between the blood loss and the use of my magic to transport us, I was so lightheaded I thought I might pass out.

I glanced around, trying to find something I could use

to hit her, but my gaze landed on a shimmering figure with a finger up to her lips.

Esme.

She nodded at me as if to say—I could do this.

I thought back to all the times in foster care the bigger kids would try to wrestle me. I had always come out on top.

I channeled that energy—that anger—into my movement, pulling my legs up and wrapping them around Darla's head and neck, then slamming her back onto the floor.

As she cried out in pain, I rose to my feet and grabbed the knife from the floor. "Don't move."

"Go ahead and kill me like you killed him. That's the only way to protect your precious friends."

"Ellie didn't kill him," Andrea said, walking past Esme from the living room. "I did."

"I knew it," I said, weakness from blood loss taking over my body. "How did you lie to the board?"

Andrea didn't respond to me.

"You killed Monroe?" Darla asked. "I thought you were friends."

"Friends?" Andrea laughed. "I guess I was a better actress than I thought."

"What?" I asked. "You and Susan were best friends."

Andrea ignored me again.

"You didn't have to kill him," Darla said.

"He deserved to die," Andrea said.

I couldn't keep my eyes open any longer. "I need help," I squeaked out.

"Don't move," Andrea said. "Renée will be here soon to heal you."

"She won't be here in time," Esme whispered in my ear. "May I?"

I nodded once before I lost consciousness.

32

When I woke up, it was dark outside. Penelope and I were tucked into my bed. Harriet was curled up in a chair with Wix at her feet.

Penelope oinked up at me.

"I'm okay," I said, examining my arm. "Esme must have healed me."

"I did," Esme's voice said through the dark.

I glanced to the other side of the bed and could faintly make out her silhouette. It sparkled in the tiny bit of moonlight peeking through the window.

"Thank you."

She placed an icy hand on my cheek. "You were smart bringing Darla here."

I smiled. "I wish we could have been together when you were alive."

"I do too," Esme said before both her silhouette and her icy touch vanished.

Harriet and Wix hadn't woken, and Penelope had

drifted back to sleep, but as hard as I tried, I could not fall back asleep.

Easing myself out of bed, I slipped on my slippers and pulled my robe off the hook behind the door.

Once I was outside the room, I carefully walked down the stairs so as not to step on the creaks.

I had an idea.

It might have been springtime, but the nighttime air hadn't quite gotten the memo. As I walked out the back door toward the barn, I pulled my robe tighter around me.

The barn was chilly but not unbearably so. I flipped on the lights and slipped behind the curtain. Why I was still tip-toeing was beyond me.

I sat on the sofa and stared up at the mural of the diner. Could it work?

I closed my eyes and concentrated.

The diner.

I want to be at the diner in the mural.

I focused my energy. My magic. It hadn't depleted like the last time. Or if it had, it had regenerated after I'd passed out.

The electricity of it buzzed through my body.

I want to be at the diner in the mural. The diner where my mother is. Emily Vanderwick.

As I said her name, I could feel the pull of energy.

It was happening.

Wind howled around me as a tornado of teleportation sucked me up.

When the world stopped spinning, I opened my eyes to find the same diner that had been in the mural.

The people in the windows moved freely, cars passed on the street behind me.

I couldn't move. Not because of anything other than fear. What if I went in there and she told me to leave?

If she didn't want to be found, what would she do if she was?

Dread crept up my neck, and I knew my hair was changing colors, but I didn't want to waste energy to stop it. I needed the magical energy to take me and possibly Emily home.

The dread transformed into hope when I saw a flash of white hair in the window. A waitress with her back to me spoke to a couple, who smiled up at her from their table.

When she turned to speak to a single person in a window booth, my heart stopped in my chest.

It was Emily.

Emily spoke to the person in the booth as if they were good friends, her smile practically lighting up the entire place. It seemed like she was telling a story as she gestured with her hands and tipped her head back to laugh.

She was beautiful.

Tingles tickled my scalp as emotion flowed through me. That was my mother. She was okay. More than okay, she seemed to be thriving.

But why hadn't she come back for me? Or gone back to see Esme?

As she returned to the counter, the person in the booth stood and walked toward the door.

She waved as the door opened.

"I'll see you next week," the man said back into the diner.

She smiled and mouthed that she was looking forward to it.

When he turned toward the parking lot, my stomach dropped.

The man speaking to my mother like an old friend was Xander.

My Xander.

Well, not *my* Xander, but Xander Wix—Laura's Xander.

He didn't see me staring as he threw a leg over his motorcycle and slid the helmet onto his head.

Anger flooded my chest. Xander swore he'd tell me the second he knew my mother's whereabouts. And here he was on what looked like a weekly coffee date with her.

Is that what was going on? Were Xander and Emily having an affair? Were they in a relationship?

I glanced back at the diner, but Emily was no longer in view of the windows.

I was about to march in and demand answers, but when Xander's headlights turned in my direction, I panicked and teleported back home.

I couldn't be sure if he'd seen me. How stupid was I to teleport back home? I summoned my magic to go back, but nothing happened. Exhaustion flooded my body.

I glanced up at the mural. It was no longer the diner. Now it was the farm, house, and barn.

As I pushed to my feet, I nearly fell over with dizziness. "No," I said to the wall. "This can't be happening. Why did it change?" I ran my hands over the paint, trying to find a speck of magic somewhere. Anywhere.

I had to go back. I had to talk to Emily.

But try as I might, I couldn't teleport.

The mural stayed static with the barn, the house, and the farm. No figures of humans or animals were included.

I pushed off the wall and plopped back on the sofa. I didn't have to feel the chill in the air or see the shimmer to know Esme was there.

"I saw her," I said, tears stinging my eyes. "I saw Emily."

"And?" I could hear the hesitation in her voice. "Is she okay?"

"She seemed just fine," I said. "Good, even. Happy."

"Did you speak to her?" Esme asked.

"No," I said. "But Xander was there, too. He spoke to her. It seemed like they were pretty good friends."

"Xander was there? How can that be? Surely, he would have told you by now."

I shrugged. "I guess I just can't trust him."

Esme didn't reply.

We sat in silence for a long time. I may have dozed off, but I couldn't be sure.

When the barn door burst open, I nearly came out of my skin.

I turned to find Katie, Fran, Amy, Bonnie, and Nancy with huge smiles on their faces.

"Hey, ladies," I said, trying my best to smile back. "I don't think I'm up for yoga this morning."

"We don't care about yoga," Katie said. "We're here to tell you that you won Mayor for a Day!"

After everything I'd been through the past couple of

days, a few trash cans seemed like a ridiculous waste of time. "Give it to Laura. I don't want it."

All of their faces dropped into frowns.

"You don't want it?" Amy asked. "But everyone voted for you. It was a landslide."

"You can't just not want it now," Katie said, moving to sit next to me on the sofa. "What happened? Why do you look like you're about to throw up?"

"It was a rough night," I said. "Can you just tell Nick to buy some trash cans on my behalf? And hire people to deal with emptying them? It really shouldn't require my presence."

Katie looked back at the other women, who shrugged, unsure what to say to me.

"On second thought," I said. "Why don't you ask him to buy one trash can and the staff to empty that one trash can, then take the rest of the budget that I would have spent on trash cans and let Laura buy some of her decorations? The decorations should come first. They're more important than trash cans."

"But you won," Bonnie said.

"Do I need to claim my sash or something?" I asked.

"There's no sash," Katie said.

"Then just let Laura take over," I said. "I don't care."

Katie gave me her best mom look. "Young lady, you will finish this. You will get off this sofa, get your butt in the shower, put on fresh clothes, and go down to the town hall to be this town's Mayor for a Day."

"Fine," I said, pushing up to a stand like a teenager who had just been told to clean their room.

ndrea rode along with me in Mona to the Mayor's office.

"Did you really kill them?" I asked.

Andrea shook her head. "You almost gave me away last night with Darla."

"Why did you tell her you killed them if you didn't?"

"I wanted her anger directed at me and not you. My job is to protect you," she said. "Simple as that."

"But if you didn't, who did?"

Andrea shrugged. "No idea."

"Come on," I said. "You have to have some idea. When you left for lunch, why did you leave the two of them alone together?"

"I had to answer a phone call." Andrea didn't look at me when I glanced over.

"From who?"

"It was a job offer, okay?" Andrea said. "It has nothing to do with this, other than my stupidity probably got my best friend killed."

Her gaze turned out the window.

"Who was the job offer from? I didn't realize guardians could get other jobs."

"You can't tell the board about this, okay?"

"I wouldn't dream of it," I said.

"Because I turned the offer down and decided to stay on as a guardian."

"Cross my heart and hope to die," I said. "Well, not really. I don't want to die. But I won't say anything. Promise."

"It was from Bell Industries in Chicago. They have a private guardian service for wealthy witches and warlocks." She sighed. "It doesn't matter, anyway. I'm happier here."

"Don't you think Darla might tell someone you killed Susan and Deacon?" I asked.

"I've been cleared," Andrea said. "Plus, I was under the truth spell in that meeting, too. I wouldn't have been able to lie."

Something felt strange, but I couldn't put a finger on it.

Either way, I didn't have time to think about it.

Nick and several townspeople stood on the sidewalk with a banner that read—*Welcome, Mayor Vanderwick!*

I couldn't help but smile as they all congratulated me.

Nick was the first to greet me, handing me a gigantic cardboard key. "The key to the city is all yours."

Cameras flashed as Coral directed them. "Olivia, come over here. Get this angle."

A woman with a shiny new camera moved to stand next to Coral.

"Ellie, look this way and smile." Coral demonstrated a massive smile, opening her eyes wide and raising her eyebrows.

"Do I know you from somewhere?" I asked Olivia.

She met my gaze and shook her head.

She looked so familiar. "Are you sure we've never met?"

"I'm positive," Olivia said in a high-pitched voice.

My chest constricted. The pieces started clicking into place. I *had* met her. At the funeral. She was the woman in pink with the high-pitched voice and the initials O.B.— Olivia Bell.

"She did it," I whispered to myself. "They did it."

"Who did what?" Nick asked.

I turned to Andrea. "One—or both of them—killed Monroe and Susan."

Andrea furrowed her brow, thinking.

"We need a big smile over here," Coral said, her voice slightly irritated.

I ignored Coral and whispered to Andrea, "You were at the funeral, right?"

Andrea nodded.

"Did you see the woman on stage before me? The one in pink who said Monroe deserved to die?"

"Maybe." Andrea scrunched up her face in concentration.

"That's her," I said. "Coral's sister is the one who blew up Monroe's coffin. Probably to destroy any extra evidence."

"Is there a problem over here?" Coral said, now only inches from me.

"Did you kill Monroe and Susan?" I asked, turning around.

"That's ridiculous," Coral said, then turned to Olivia. "I'm calling our father so he can call the attorneys. Don't say anything, she's with the police."

Olivia stood holding her camera with an unsure look on her face.

"That's an awfully nice camera, it looks new," I said.

"I'm a photographer," Olivia said. "I have a lot of cameras."

"Why did you blow up Monroe's body?" I asked Olivia. "Were you trying to get rid of any evidence that might still incriminate your sister?"

"Yes, this is Coral Bell. I need to speak to my father," Coral said. "Don't answer her question, Olivia."

Olivia shifted her weight.

"Your last name is Bell," I said. "As in Bell Industries in Chicago?"

Recognition dawned on Andrea's face. "The call with the job offer was fake. You set it up to get me out of the way, didn't you?"

"It's not what you think," Olivia said.

"Then what is it?" I asked. "If you're honest, it'll be much better for you."

"She only wanted me to catch them in a compromising position," Olivia said.

"Shut up, Olivia," Coral said.

But Olivia didn't do as her sister commanded. "Coral set up the call to get you away from the two of them. I followed them into the bathroom with my camera, but h-he—"

"That is enough." Coral stepped between Olivia and me.

"Did Monroe try to hurt you?" I asked. "What was he doing?"

"Dad, we need your attorney in the Cliff Haven square immediately," Coral shouted into the phone. "No, ten minutes is too long. Olivia's trying to get us both arrested."

I looked past Coral at Olivia. "What was Monroe doing?"

Coral tried to step between us again, but Olivia stepped around her. "Quit," Olivia said. "I need to tell them what happened."

"Fine, but keep my name out of your mouth," Coral said. "If you're going to go down with a bang, don't take me with you."

"That's impossible," Olivia said, tears gathering in her eyes. "You were there the entire time. It doesn't matter. It was all in self-defense. You don't go to jail for self-defense."

Coral looked like she might deck her sister.

"Start at the beginning," I said gently to Olivia as Andrea tried to keep Coral from attacking.

"We knew Susan and Monroe were having an affair, but Andrea always seemed to be with them." Olivia took a deep breath. "Coral set up a call for Andrea after she applied for a job with our family company. When Andrea was out of the way, I followed Susan and Monroe into the bathroom. I snapped a few photos before I realized they weren't doing what I thought they were."

"I assume you thought they went in there to hook up?" I asked.

"Right, that's why I was taking photos," Olivia said. "But when I realized what I was taking photos of, I freaked. He was strangling her. I didn't know what to do, so I threw my camera at him."

That explained the shards of camera lens we found at the crime scene.

Andrea had successfully gotten Coral calmed down. They both listened to Olivia's confession.

"What happened then?"

"Monroe came after me. That's where I got the bruises on my forearms," Olivia said, glancing at Coral. "But then Coral came in, pulled out her gun, and shot him. It was self-defense. She didn't kill him because she wanted to. We knew what he was capable of. If she wouldn't have shot him, he would have killed me like he killed Susan."

"Why didn't you call the police and tell them what happened?" I asked. "Why did you tamper with the crime scene?"

Olivia looked down at her feet. "We didn't want bad publicity for our family, so we set it up to look like a murder-suicide."

"And you blew up the body because of potential evidence?" I asked.

She nodded in confirmation.

Andrea pulled out two pairs of handcuffs. "Coral and Olivia Bell, you're under arrest."

"But why?" Olivia asked. "I just told you—it was self-defense. It was my life or his."

"The courts will have to determine all that," Andrea said.

"Even if they don't, our attorneys will get us out of it," Coral said. "Our father pays them good money for things like this."

Andrea led them away as the cameras shifted from me and flashed in their direction.

"Do not photograph us," Coral shouted. "This is not why you're here."

Nick cleared his throat. "Mayor Vanderwick, will you do the honors?" He held up a large cardboard door with a keyhole big enough for the key I didn't remember I was holding.

The people on either side of him clapped slowly.

I did my best to smile after what had just happened. "Thank you for voting for me. I have decided to dedicate a small portion of my budget to one trash can and the staff to service that trash can."

"Only one?" Nick asked. "But what about the rest of the budget?"

"It should go to decorations—under Laura's supervision." I glanced around. "Is she here?"

Nick shook his head. "She thought it'd be better not to come."

"Understandable." I slid the key into the cardboard door lock and turned.

The townspeople clapped again.

"If that's what you've decided," Nick said. "Let's go write up the budgetary changes. We can present them at the town meeting together."

"Does that mean I'm invited to the town meetings?"

"I suppose it does," Nick said.

Andrea returned to my side. "That was good detective work, Ellie. I'm impressed."

"Thanks," I said. "Have you seen Xander? I need to talk to him. I would guess he's with Laura."

Andrea and Nick exchanged a knowing look.

"What?" I asked.

"I'm surprised you hadn't heard," she said. "Xander and Laura broke up. He left town last night."

"They broke up?" I asked. "How? Why?"

"She made a big deal in the middle of the festival over how magic is dangerous, and she could have died," Nick said. "Xander tried to calm her down, but she was hysterical. Screaming and such. When she yelled at him that it was over, he got on his motorcycle and drove away."

"No one has seen him since," Andrea said.

That wasn't completely true.

I'd seen him since.

With my mother at the diner.

And now, I needed to find him and figure out what was really going on.

Right after I completed my one mayoral day.

Thank you so much for reading *Festival Fiasco*!

Don't miss Ellie's next adventure—*Justice Jamboree*!

.   .   .

If you enjoyed Festival Fiasco and want to leave a review on Amazon/ Goodreads/ Bookbub/ Blog/ Social Media, that would be amazing! Reviews help other readers choose which books to spend their time reading! You can also tell your friends about it too!

Also, I love hearing from readers! Email me at stellabixbyauthor@gmail.com.

ACKNOWLEDGMENTS

Thank You, God. These past few months have been a challenge for my writing, but I know You were with me the entire time.

Thank you to my readers. You make me want to be better and faster every single day.

My betas, I say it every time, but you make my books what they are. Thank you for all your help.

My ARC team—you're amazing! Without you, my books would not be nearly as successful as they are. Thank you.

My family and friends—your support is everything. When I struggle, you're there to give me encouragement, grace, and love. Thank you so much. I love you all.

ABOUT THE AUTHOR

Stella Bixby is a native Coloradan who loves to snowboard, pluck at the guitar, and play board games with her family. She was once a volunteer firefighter and a park ranger, but now spends most of her time making up stories and trying to figure out what to cook for dinner.

Connect with Stella on Facebook, Twitter, and Instagram @StellaBixby.

Stella loves to hear from her readers!
www.stellabixby.com

ALSO BY STELLA BIXBY

Novels:

Rylie Cooper Series

Catfished: Book 1

Suckered: Book 2

Throttled: Book 3

Tampered: Book 4

Whacked: Book 5

Bungled: Book 6

Snowed: Book 7

Magical Mane Mystery Series

Downward Death: Book 1

Bowling Blunder: Book 2

Spotlight Scandal: Book 3

Tango Trouble: Book 4

Spelunking Speculations: Book 5

Festival Fiasco: Book 6